NEVER SHOOT A VAMPIRE

▼▼

The bullet lanced my chest like a white-hot needle, its impact and effect all out of proportion to its size. His aim was perfect, precise as a top surgeon's. It went in just left of my breastbone, slipped between the ribs to clip my heart, and tore out my back.

Time slowed and movement along with it. As a sound separate from the shot, I heard the flat *tink* of lead on steel as it struck one of the barrels behind me. Before the finger could tighten on the trigger again, I was on him. His lips peeled back as I wrenched the gun away, a mirror of my own pain. The bullet's tearing flight through my body had nearly knocked me down from the fire-red shock.

I wanted him to feel the same hurt, I wanted him to know about death . . .

THE VAMPIRE FILES

Don't miss Jack Fleming's three previous adventures—*Bloodlist*, *Lifeblood*, and *Bloodcircle*—a thrilling saga of blood and passion as only a vampire could tell it.

"A sharp vampire's-eye view . . . excellent."
—*Dragon* Magazine

"Fast . . . intriguing!" —*Midwest Book Review*

The Vampire Files

BOOK FOUR

ART IN THE BLOOD

P.N. ELROD

ACE BOOKS, NEW YORK

ART IN THE BLOOD

An Ace Book / published by arrangement with
the author

PRINTING HISTORY
Ace edition / February 1991

ISBN: 0-441-85945-3

Ace Books are published by The Berkley Publishing Group,
200 Madison Avenue, New York, New York 10016.
The name "ACE" and the "A" logo
are trademarks belonging to Charter Communications, Inc.

PRINTED IN THE UNITED STATES OF AMERICA

10 9 8 7 6 5 4 3 2 1

"Art in the blood is liable to take the strangest forms."

—Sherlock Holmes, in *The Adventure of the Greek Interpreter* by A. Conan Doyle

ART IN THE BLOOD

HUNGRY AND CARELESS, I'd opened the vein more than necessary and the blood slipped past my mouth and dribbled down the animal's leg. I shifted my right hand above the wound and applied pressure, which slowed the flow, and continued with my meal, siphoning off more than usual because I'd been on short rations the last few nights. I drank my fill and more, the excess partly due to curiosity; I wanted to know if I'd swell up like a leech or if I could get away with fewer feedings per week. The cow didn't mind, she could afford to spare a quart or more—there'd just be that much less to spill out when they finally slaughtered her for someone else's dinner.

I drew away, a handkerchief immediately at my lips so as not to spot my clothes, and tightened the pressure on the leg. It worked, and the bleeding eventually stopped. My hand looked the same, at least—no puffiness there. I wondered how long it would take for the red to fade from my eyes. The usual time was only a few minutes, but there was no way to tell. These days I preferred to avoid useless mirrors and their many complications.

To spare my shoes from farmyard-style damage, I went incorporeal to get out and flowed past the wood corrals and their complaining occupants. It was a disorienting state, but I knew the route well and was soon back on the open street again, doing my best imitation of a normal man out for a walk. My car was parked less than a block away, but I always varied my route into and out of the Stockyards. Few people believed in vampires these days, but it never hurt to be careful.

The first aid to the cow had stained my fingers somewhat, so I took a swing past Escott's office with a mind to borrow his washroom. His lights were on, which surprised me, for only yesterday he'd mentioned a dearth of business. I didn't feel like his company just then and kept walking, but silently wished him luck as I passed. He detested being idle. A dripping tap in an alley down the street provided all the cleanup I needed, and I tossed the stained handkerchief into a trash can. Escott's laundry service, which I shared now, had once asked if his houseguest suffered from frequent nosebleeds.

The car started up without fuss and I drove aimlessly, turning when the mood struck me and obeying the stop signals like a good citizen. I pulled up and parked near the Night-crawler Club up on the north side and pretended it was only an impulse that took me there, and not some inner need.

They had a new man out front. He looked askance at my ordinary clothes, but let me in when I asked to see Gordy. The hatcheck girl was not new, I rarely forget dimples, but she didn't know me from whosis, and put my plain gray fedora next to the flashier silk toppers with a friendly if impersonal smile.

I knew the place had been raided by the cops at least once since my last visit, and Gordy had taken the temporary shutdown as an opportunity to redecorate. The walls were bright with fresh paint, and the tables, chairs, and bandstand were now shiny black with gleaming chrome trim. The only thing unchanged were the costumes on the girls, which remained black with silver-sequined spiderwebs patterned on the happily short skirts. The leggy details were enough to keep me occupied until Gordy showed up.

He was puzzled to see me, maybe slightly wary as well, but when I stuck my hand out he took it. He was a big mountain of a man with a solid, but not crushing grip. He had no need to prove his strength against anyone, taking it for granted people could figure it out for themselves.

" 'Lo, Fleming, what's up?"

"This and that. Got a quieter place than here?" I gestured at the band across the dance floor below. They were just starting off another tune for the patrons.

He nodded, not one for much wordage, and led the way through a door marked Private. The soundproofing did its job and we were in the casino room, up to our eyeballs in stale smoke and the tight atmosphere of prolonged tension. Gordy nodded to a couple of tough boys in tuxedos guarding the money cage and threaded through the craps and roulette tables to the back exit. We took a short hall and some stairs up to an office I remembered very well. The redecorating had gotten this far with a new rug, paint, and paintings. His deceased boss's boats had been replaced by green-and-brown pastorals. A canvas depicting a lush forest covered a section of the wall where six slugs from a .38 had embedded themselves one memorable night.

"Nice picture, huh?" he said, noticing my interest. There was a very slight humor coming from his eyes. "I like to look at it."

"That's what they're there for." I noticed it was not an ordinary store-bought print, but a real oil with a decent frame.

"Yeah."

He pointed at a deep leather chair and settled into a wide matching sofa, taking up most of it. He wasn't fat, just big, and I knew from experience he could move fast and light when he wanted to; the present slowness was all part of his camouflage. Large men were supposed to be slow and stupid, so Gordy cultivated that image and thus kept a lot of people off balance. In his business an edge always came in handy.

"Want anything?" he asked, meaning refreshments.

I shook my head and with some caution removed my dark glasses. From his reaction I could tell my eyes were still quite red from the feeding.

"You look like you had a hell of a weekend."

"I did."

"You're not the social type, Fleming, at least for places like this and mugs like me. You got a problem?"

"Yeah."

He apparently recalled the last time he'd seen my bloodred eyes. "Trouble with Bobbi?"

"No."

"Another woman?"

I couldn't tell if he was being perceptive like Escott or if it was simply the next logical question for him to ask. "Yeah, you could say that."

"What kind of trouble?"

"I killed her."

The news didn't exactly send him into a panic. "You need protection, a cleanup job?"

"No, nothing like that."

He had one of those phlegmatic faces under his short-cropped blond hair; great for poker or making people sweat. "You need to talk about it?"

My instinct to come see him had been right, and I nodded, inwardly relieved.

"So talk," he said. He wasn't the soul of encouragement, but he settled back into the depths of the sofa to listen. I gave him a short version of how I'd killed the young woman and why I'd done it, just stating bald facts and not bothering with any defense. During the story he stared at yet another painting above and behind his desk, his eyes hardly blinking the whole time.

"I'm sure Charles knows about it, but he hasn't said anything. I don't think he ever will."

"Smart guy, then," he approved. "What about Barrett?"

"He apparently took the suicide at face value."

"He probably wants to. How are you taking it?"

"I feel like . . ." But I couldn't finish. I couldn't put words to what I was feeling.

He raised a hand to call off the question and tried another. "You remember the war?"

"I was in it."

This confused him, since I didn't look old enough, but he continued. "You fight? You have to kill?"

"Yeah, I see what you're getting at. This was different."

"Why? Because it was a woman and in a nice house and not out in a field of mud with the noise and cold? She was killing people. You had to stop her. What's the problem?"

"Living with it. Why me?"

He shifted his sleepy-looking eyes from me back to the painting. It was a soft overview of a farm near sunset, in one corner a boy was leading two plow horses back to the stable. "When I was a kid, I once knew a retired hangman. I asked him about it. He knew how to do it better than anyone else but he didn't think much about it, it was just a job to do. I can't say he enjoyed it, but he knew he was doing his part in making things cleaner."

It seemed an odd statement coming from him, considering how he came by his living. "Yeah?"

"Yeah. You either learn to live with it or you go crazy. Make up your mind."

"Is that what you've done?"

He glanced over, again with faint humor. "I'm just a businessman."

"That's what Capone used to say."

"Huh. He never talked about the dirty side of the business, not where he could be overheard. He'd pretend it wasn't there. Maybe that makes him crazy. I know it's there, I don't enjoy it, but I'm good at it. And I'm not crazy."

The humor was more pronounced, but under it was something hard and very cold. The base of my spine went stiff as I suppressed a shiver.

A few days, or nights, later I was just coming down from the upstairs bath when I heard Escott let himself in the kitchen door. His arms were full with a newspaper, raincoat, and several small cartons, and the latchkey got stuck in the lock again. When he started to jiggle it loose he nearly lost the cartons. Drawing a breath to say hello I caught a strong whiff of Chinese food and rushed to rescue the soggy white boxes before his dinner ended up on the floor.

"Thank you," he said as I transferred them to the counter by the sink. He extracted his key and glared at the lock for exactly one second, tossed his coat and hat on the table, and stalked into the dining room. He was back almost immediately with a screwdriver and small oil can, and began an energetic assault on the rusty mechanism.

"Your dinner'll get cold," I said, leaning against a doorway to watch the show.

"A distinct possibility, but I'd rather it be cold than suffer the indigestion this recalcitrant lock is likely to cause me."

"You almost make me glad I've given up eating."

His mouth twitched, whether from amusement at my remark or frustration at the job was hard to tell. Something gave, and he seized the oil can and attacked the breach in the lock's defense while it was vulnerable. He experimented with the key, grunted with satisfaction, and put things back the way they were.

"Good evening, Jack," he said, standing and dusting his knees off. It was his way of starting things over fresh. "How are you tonight?" His suit coat joined the raincoat on the table and he turned on the hot water in the sink to wash his hands.

"Fine. You look tired."

"Thank you so much. I can assure you it is not from overwork."

"You were busy the last few nights."

"Yes, but that little—extremely little—job is resolved and I've nothing to do now."

"Boredom?" I knew how exhausting that could get.

"Inactivity. I never allow myself to become bored, but inactivity may strike at any inconvenient moment."

"There's a difference?"

He registered mock surprise as he toweled dry. "Most certainly. One cannot help inactivity, but boredom is a self-inflicted disease. I firmly believe there is a special Providence watching us all for signs of boredom, the moment we declare ourselves in that state some disaster will occur to take our minds right out of it. The last time I was bored was the year 1920. I was carrying a spear, so to speak, in the court of King Claudius. . . ."

I looked blank.

"*Hamlet*?" he suggested, by way of clarification.

Dawn broke. "You were on stage in front of an audience and bored? I'd be scared to death."

"Given time, one can become used to anything. I'd grown all too familiar with that particular scene in that particular play and thus declared myself bored. The next thing I knew the trapdoor we used for the Ghost to enter from under the stage gave way and down I went. It was one of my more spectacular exits."

"Were you hurt?"

"A bruise or two when I landed on the platform below had me limping for a week. It seems the fellow playing the Ghost forgot to latch the trap properly after his last scene."

"Did you kill him?"

"He was terribly embarrassed so I thought it more vengeful not to put him out of his misery." He pulled out a few clean plates and emptied the cartons onto them. "Since then I've schooled myself to patience when it comes to inactivity. I've completely sworn off boredom."

I shoved his things to one side of the table to give him room. "So work is slow?"

"I more than caught up on my reading." He nodded at the crumpled newspaper.

"Not even a divorce to turn away?"

His thin lips curled in distaste. "Please, I am about to eat."

"Sorry."

"What social event are you off to tonight?" he asked in turn as his long fingers snapped up a set of chopsticks with practiced ease.

"How did you—"

"You've taken more care than usual with your hair, that is a new shirt and tie, and I believe Miss Smythe will be quite impressed with the after-shave and shoe shine."

"Looks okay, then? I can't really tell."

"Mirrors must be a considerable source of annoyance to you these days."

"You can say that again," I grumbled.

"The event?" he repeated, just before plunging into his chow mein or whatever it was; the smell was making me vaguely nauseous, but that was my usual reaction to solid, cooked food.

"Some kind of party. Bobbi and Marza got a job singing and playing background music, and their boss said it was okay to bring a date."

"It sounds an odd mix of the formal and informal."

"Yeah, bunch of artists up along the north shore. One of them's loaded and wants plenty of people along to celebrate a show he's having at his fiancée's gallery."

"His name?"

"Leighton Brett."

His right eyebrow bounced once and he indicated the paper with his chopsticks. "Page eight."

I uncrumpled it and opened to the page. It was a splashy article placed above the fold with lots of photos. A picture of Brett standing with some people took up most of the space. It was a standard pose of him shaking hands; in the background was some kind of landscape painting. The caption said he'd won the Lloyd A. Farron Medal and five hundred dollars for a painting called *Homeward Bound*. Brett was a big man, towering over the others by a head. He had a long, solemn face, dark, curly hair, and serious eyes.

Another photo of him with his fiancée Reva Stokes had them standing before his portrait of her. He was accurate and had caught her looks exactly right, but somehow softened and sweetened them so at second glance it seemed like a different woman from the cool-faced blond next to him.

The article went into detail about Brett's award presentation and the opening of his own gallery. Reva would be managing the sales; his job was to keep the place filled with new work. The between-the-lines message indicated he was destined to be one of art's new masters and consequently a good investment for collectors.

I went back to the first photo, drawn by something familiar in the painting. It looked very much like the farm scene hanging above Gordy's desk. This one still had a boy leading two plow horses, but the stable was gone, replaced by trees and part of a dirt road.

"This painting"—I pointed out *Homeward Bound*— "Gordy's got an almost identical one in his office."

"You've been to see Gordy?" He was mildly surprised.

"Just to say hello. I'll have to ask him who the artist is."

"It could be Brett, I understand he's quite prolific."

"But why paint the same scene twice?"

He shrugged. "You could ask him. More than once da Vinci did two versions of one scene. *The Virgin of the Rocks* comes to mind, and *La Gioconda*." He rolled the foreign word out with dramatic relish and attacked his rice.

"La what?"

"The *Mona Lisa*, my dear fellow."

"There's only one *Mona Lisa*."

"In the Louvre. There's another sitting quietly in a bank vault in New York. It's a shocking waste."

"You're pulling my leg."

"I assure you it is absolutely genuine."

"How come no one's ever heard of it, then?"

"Because the owners want no part of the attitude of disbelief, which you are presently displaying with such clarity, or to attract the attention of potential thieves."

"How do you know about it?"

"I read a lot," he said, but I picked up a note in his voice that indicated he was skirting the truth. Before I could jump out with another question, he glanced up at the kitchen clock. "Perhaps this is forward of me, but I noted in the story about Leighton Brett that the party he is having tonight begins at eight, and it is just now—"

"Holy shit." I ran down to the basement and grabbed my hat and coat. To save time I vanished and reappeared in the kitchen, a stunt that often unnerved Escott. It worked. He nearly choked on his bean sprouts, but recovered beautifully.

"Shall I leave the latch off?" he asked dryly, knowing full well I had no problems with locked doors.

"Nah, but don't wait up for me."

He tossed my wry look back and saluted me out with a wave of his chopsticks.

Traffic wasn't good, but I was less anxious for my own lateness than Bobbi's; I had no wish to cost her a job. I rounded the last corner to the front of her residence hotel and saw them already outside looking for me; Bobbi, her accompanist Marza Chevreaux, and Marza's date, Madison Pruitt. Bobbi opened the passenger door and swooped inside to plant a quick kiss on me before Marza could scowl disapproval.

"Sorry I'm late," I said.

"You're timing's always been perfect for me," she whispered with a little smirk, and then Marza and Madison were piling into the backseat. Marza did have something acid to say about my lateness, but Bobbi's last remark had my head swimming, so I didn't hear any of it.

Bobbi brought out a much-folded scrap of paper and called directions, while Madison tried to engage me in a political discussion. He had taken great stock in last Wednesday's rumor that Hitler was planning to retire and turn the chancelorship over to his air minister, Goering. I didn't see that it would make much difference, but all the way along Michigan Avenue he argued passionately in favor of keeping Hitler in charge of things.

"I thought the Communists didn't like Hitler," I ventured when he paused for breath.

"We don't, but Goering would be worse. He's better educated and a trained military leader. As soon as they finish practicing in Spain his air force is going to be bombing Paris next. Don't forget the German army moved into the Rhineland Zone only last March—"

Marza finished for him. "—and next thing you know they'll be using the Eiffel Tower for target practice. We've heard it all before, Madison."

"But Jack hasn't. Have you?"

"I'm always interested in hearing people's opinions."

In the mirror I saw Marza shoot the back of my head a look that would have done Medusa credit, and Madison continued with his political observations for the rest of the trip. Occasionally, he even seemed to make sense. Bobbi kept us on course until we were in the middle of what I would call a rich neighborhood, and counted off house numbers. The one we wanted took up an entire block and was lit up like New Year's.

"Look at the cars," said Marza. "We're late."

"They're early," Bobbi corrected. "Reva said there'd be some hangers-on from the gallery opening."

"I'll drop you at the front and park the buggy," I suggested. "No sense in all of us taking a hike."

"They should have hired some valets," said Marza, still wanting to stew.

Madison snorted. "And lose their image as unworldly artists?"

"Darling, anyone who lives in a pile of such proportions has a very clear idea of how the world works, and it certainly would not have stretched their budget much to provide a little basic comfort to their guests." Marza had apparently forgotten she was at the party to work, not play. Bobbi glanced at me and managed to keep a straight face.

The exterior of the house was comfortably ugly, built of large slabs of gray stone in the shape of a mock castle, complete with a crenelated roofline. The grounds were formal and well kept, with only a few early leaves skittering in the wind over the gray brick driveway. I paused under a huge covered entry to unload the others, then rolled out again to find a parking space. Space found, I strolled back up the drive with a few other arrivals. Some were in formal clothes and looking smug about it; another group was dressed for an afternoon in the yacht basin and looking equally pleased with themselves. I overheard one of the formals also complain about the lack of parking valets, but no one else seemed to mind.

Bobbi was waiting in the entry for me and slipped a possessive arm through mine.

"What happened to—" I started.

"Madison spotted some friends and dragged Marza along inside. For all his dad's money you'd think he could afford to buy some manners."

"Or even rent them. Don't worry about it, Madison's still a kid."

"He's over thirty."

"There are kids and then there are kids. Have I told you how gorgeous you are tonight?"

"Not out loud, but feel free to—oomph . . ."

She said to feel free, which is why I grabbed her and kissed her, garnering a few whoops of encouragement from a clutch of passing guests. Despite the distractions, Bobbi didn't put up any fight and gave as good as she got.

"When does the party end?" I asked.

She took a deep breath. "Five minutes from now would be too long, but hold that thought."

I grinned back, and we assumed a more sedate posture and walked inside.

The windows were wide open, but insufficient to the task of cooling down the rapidly crowding room. Brightly clad bodies, cigarette smoke, and the steady rumble of conversation filled all the corners, and this was just the front hall. I automatically looked for a familiar face and was mildly surprised to spot one, though I'd never met her before. Reva Stokes, slim, self-possessed, and carefully dressed in a shade of chocolate brown that matched her eyes, broke away from a conversation, extending a long hand at Bobbi.

"So glad to see you, Miss Smythe." Her voice was smooth with a touch of throat to it. Bobbi introduced me as her date and asked where she was to sing.

"The long hall, I'll take you there." She turned and led the way, talking over her shoulder. "It's the largest room we have, but I'm afraid the acoustics are terrible. Leighton refused to have the piano moved."

"I'm sure it will be fine. The gallery opening went well, I hope?"

"Oh, yes, just wonderful." She sounded anything but enthused.

Bobbi was nerved up enough to hold my hand all the way there. The long hall had fewer people in it, but the twenty-foot ceiling and bare floor turned it into a cross between an echo chamber and a bowling alley. I never did notice the walls for all the humanity in the way.

Folding chairs and music stands were arranged to one side of a grand piano the size of my Buick. Several men in tuxedos were sorting through some sheet music and tuning their instruments. Reva asked them to start the background music as soon as they could and told Bobbi she could pick her own program. A white-haired man in the back spotted Bobbi, broke into a smile of greeting, and came over to kiss her cheek.

"Bobbi, you look wonderful as always. Now who's the tall fellow getting so jealous?"

"Titus, this is my date, Jack Fleming. Jack, this is Titus Noble, leader of the band."

Noble pretended to wince. "String quartet, my dear girl."

He glad-handed me. "I remember you from Bobbi's house-warming party. Marza said you were in the rackets."

"Titus!"

"Bobbi, if I don't ask questions, I'll never learn anything. The hard part is surviving the answers. Well, Mr. Fleming?"

"Jack," I said automatically. "And sorry if it disappoints you, but I'm not."

He craned his neck to one of the other musicians. "Teddy, you owe me a beer. Then what do you do besides escort beautiful young singers around to places like this?"

"I'm a writer." My answer popped out naturally and hopefully covered out-of-work journalists like myself.

"Ohhh." He nodded a bit vaguely, then leaned close to Bobbi's ear. "Don't marry him until he has at least three best-sellers under his belt."

She cuffed his arm playfully, then they started hashing out the music program for the evening. They didn't get far before realizing they'd need Marza. I volunteered to go look for her and started weaving through the knots of chattering people and waiters balancing silver trays.

She was with Madison, who was holding forth before a group of Bohemian types on his favorite subject: the unfairness of the world in general, and how Marx had given them all a blueprint on how to make things work. Marza looked bored to death, and if she didn't exactly welcome my interruption with open arms she had no insults ready, either. I told her where Bobbi was and she walked off—rather quickly. I listened for another minute to the political lecture, decided he'd ceased to make sense again, and drifted back to the main hall to watch the show.

It didn't take long for Bobbi to get things straight with Noble, who led off the music with one of those chamber things that all sound alike. I was surprised at the volume coming out of their stringed instruments, and it had an immediate quieting effect on the people closest to the players. Titus played a violin with the apparently easy concentration of a true professional, but I found it difficult to sit and listen, for some of the high notes sounded like nails on a blackboard. He was an expert enough player, but now my ears were just too damned sensitive to listen with any comfort. After a few minutes I was getting to the limit of my duration, but then the music abruptly wound up to a self-satisfied finish and everyone started applauding.

Marza gave him enough time for a decent bow, then attacked the piano keys with her maroon talons and Bobbi launched into one of her club numbers. It was a light love song and apparently a favorite, as a few more people squeezed into the room to see who was singing and then stayed because Bobbi's looks matched her voice. She was quietly dressed in a high-necked, long-sleeved gown of midnight blue, but it was some kind of soft, clingy fabric that floated and moved with her body. I was hypnotized along with the rest and didn't make a sound until she was finished and bowing to her share of the applause.

Titus took another turn, a somewhat longer piece with not much violin to it, so I was able to tolerate things. Bobbi edged away from the piano and came over to see me.

"You bite a lemon or something?" she asked.

"The music's fine, I just can't listen to it." I explained my sensitive ears and she sympathized.

"I'll tell Titus, then, or he'll think you won't like his playing. He's been worried enough about whether Reva's brainstorm would work."

"What's Reva's brainstorm? Mixing you and Titus together?"

"Right, the idea is to give everyone something they like. I think it's supposed to reflect her husband's painting style."

"Any of his stuff hanging around? I'd like to see it."

"Probably. Find a wall if you can and follow it. I'll have a break in about thirty minutes. . . ."

"I'll be back."

She squeezed my hand and returned to the chair reserved for her next to Marza, who was pretending to study her sheet music.

Madison appeared next to me, a disappointing and depressing substitute at best. He shook his head at the general direction of the players and sighed. "What a waste of money."

"People gotta have music."

"Don't you see, though? Look at the way the world is and

tell me we couldn't fix things if we could develop a classless society to spread the wealth around."

"Probably," I agreed with caution. "But it would only work if everyone was in it on a voluntary basis and stuck to it."

"That's what I'm trying to do, only sometimes it seems impossible."

"You get that as long as you deal with people. Everyone's got an opinion and they generally think theirs is right."

"But I *am* right!"

"Keep your voice down, you don't want to get thrown out and us with you."

He calmed down very little, grinding his teeth in time to the music. "You hungry?" he asked, lighting on a fresh subject, no doubt inspired by the close passage of a waiter with a tray.

"Nah, you go ahead." And he was gone before I'd finished speaking. The quartet piece ended and Bobbi was up again, this time singing three in a row, finishing up with a version of "Melancholy Baby" that would stop traffic on a hot day. The hall was full up by now and more were more trying to crowd in. Bad acoustics or not, Reva had a success on her hands, if you could tell anything from the applause.

Titus started up another chamber piece and Bobbi slipped away. We couldn't get together because of all the people in between, so she pointed in the direction she planned to go and I nodded over the mass of heads.

The air got considerably cooler because a bank of French windows leading into the back garden were wide open. Bobbi went out one on her side, I used mine, and we met in the middle on the back porch.

"Thought I was going to suffocate," she said, grabbing my arm. "Let's take a walk, I need the air."

"You need a medal, you're just the greatest."

She smiled and glowed and I felt that pleasant stab hit me all over again because she was so beautiful and we were together. We didn't bother with talk and followed a winding cement path on a slow stroll. I hardly noticed the garden, getting only an impression of thick, high hedges, faint Japanese lanterns, and cast-iron furniture at convenient spots. She picked a wide seat trimmed in white-painted grapevines and sank onto it with a sigh. I sat next to her, holding her in the crook of my arm in case it was too cool for her after the pressing warmth of the hall.

"I'd like to have a place like this," she said. "A garden so big you lose yourself in it, and someone else to bring me breakfast in the afternoon."

"Don't you mean morning?"

"Not with the hours I keep. Did you mean that when you told Titus you were a writer?"

"It'll do until something else comes along."

"What do you write?"

"Your name across the sky in diamonds."

She laughed at the image, no doubt expressing her good taste.

"Would you like some?" I asked.

"What, diamonds?"

"Yeah."

She sobered. "What girl wouldn't?" But her tone was off.

"You don't like the idea?"

"I like the thought behind it, but I don't want that kind of gift—not from you."

"Why not from me?"

"Because of the way it used to be for me. I took things like that from Slick, like a fancy payment—you know I was no angel—but I don't want anything like that from you. Things are different with you, and I want them to stay that way."

She looked uncertain on how I was going to react, but I didn't have any choice in the matter. I pulled her tight and close and didn't stop kissing her until she insisted on coming up for air by thumping the back of my neck.

"Like I said," she continued, "hold that thought."

"I'll do more than that," I said, and started exploring her lips again. Her heartbeat was way up, along with her breathing.

"On the other hand, why wait?" she asked, and I paused.

"What?" Sometimes I can be pretty dim, but I caught on fast when she did something with her collar and it dropped several inches. "Oh, you can't mean here and. . . ."

"Why not? I'm ready for you now and I don't want to wait till after the party. I'll be too tired to enjoy things."

I could see her point, but felt suddenly vulnerable. The alcove we occupied didn't seem all that private. I could still hear voices uncomfortably near. She put her mouth on mine again and her arms went up my back to pull me closer.

"It's really very dark here," she whispered. "No one can see and if they do they'll just think we're necking—won't they?"

She was certainly right about that—in more ways than one—and I couldn't stop kissing her anyway. The pumping of her blood was as hypnotic to me as her voice, and I gradually sank lower along her neck until I was just over the two small marks left by our previous encounters. My canine teeth were already out and ready, but it was a new angle for me and I had to twist around a little more so I wouldn't hurt her.

She kept silent as I broke the skin, but her body went stiff and then shuddered, and she held me harder than ever as the pleasure rolled over her again and again. I drew it out for both of us, taking one seeping drop at a time. The thunder of her heartbeat and her now-languorous breathing drowned out all other sounds for me. There was only the shimmering woman in my arms and the taste of her life enriching my own.

2

BOBBI SAID MY eyes were still flushed bloodred, so I could only walk her partway back to the house. As soon as we got close to better lit areas and more people, she broke away with a smile and wave and went in to start another set. I returned to the cool solitude of the garden, found our bench again, and sat down, feeling peaceful and mellow about the world in general and quiet excitement over Bobbi in particular.

Sounds from the house drifted over the tailored grounds, the usual murmur of conversation, and the piano, then Bobbi's voice rose in plaintive song. She was having a private joke kidding me: the tune she'd chosen was "Red Sails in the Sunset." When the applause settled down, Titus Noble took over with a high-pitched string number that made the inside of my head itch. It was all part of the internal change; when I'd been a daylight walker I'd had no trouble with violin music. For self-protection I drifted farther from the house, putting trees and more hedges between my sensitive eardrums and the noise.

Sounds of another kind soon caught my attention, low voices, male, and I instinctively knew they were trying to be secretive. Their whispers were almost up to conversation level and punctuated irregularly by muffled laughter.

They were gathered at the foot of a massive fountain where a nearly naked stone woman dumped water endlessly from a jug. The big paper lanterns in the court gave them just enough light to see. A few glanced up from their circle at my approach, then turned back to the hot game of Harlem tennis they were playing against the fountain's marble base.

A youngish man with dark, sandy hair combed forward over a high brow puffed air into his fist, said a short prayer to Lady Luck, and tossed the dice with a practiced hand. They clicked and clattered on the pavement, hit against the low wall of the fountain, and bounced to a stop. The man crowed, others groaned, and money was swiftly collected, exchanged, and put down for the next toss.

Grinning broadly, he swept up the dice and breathed on them again, rubbing them between his hands with something like love.

"They're hot enough, Evan," someone complained, followed by an impatient chorus of agreement.

Evan tempered his grin and threw with an expert twist and follow-through, giving out a muted yell of triumph. More money was passed, and the rumpled stack where he knelt grew. The general opinion was that his streak couldn't last another roll and the bets were down. Evan went through more breathing exercises, rolled his eyes, and grimaced as though to transfer his hopes and energies into the dotted cubes. Silence fell on the restive group for the few seconds it took until the dice stopped and the resulting shouts of outrage and glee were enough to travel back to the house.

Just as he was collecting another rift of bills and congratulations, another man grabbed the dice over Evan's surprised protest. They scuffled, but the losers in the game got them apart, apparently aware there was a reason behind the breach of etiquette.

"What is it, Dreyer?"

The man walked under a paper lantern and looked at the dice carefully. I could almost hear him growling. He bounced them in his palm a few times, then rolled them at the base of the fountain.

"It's not your turn," complained Evan, who was just beginning to sweat.

Another man examined the results of the roll, then tossed them twice more over Evan's objections. By now Dreyer wasn't the only one growling, and Evan was facing a ring of hostile faces.

"Just a little joke, boys . . ." he said with a sick smile, hoping against hope someone would laugh.

Dreyer punched him in the stomach. He doubled over and would have fallen if not for all the supporting hands. It signaled a general free-for-all aimed at Evan and a fast scramble to recover the money. The milling bodies totally buried him for a moment, then his vague cry floated up clearly from the guttural profanity. The mass lurched and something large splashed into the fountain.

Until the punch in the stomach, I'd followed the proceedings with some amusement, good entertainment being a rare thing. After the punch I debated on just how to step in, but the splash got me moving. I was all too well acquainted with getting beaten to a pulp and dumped into water. Cheat or not, Evan had an ally.

I shoved flailing bodies out of the way to get to the fountain. It was shallow, but Evan's torso was underwater and destined to remain so as long as Dreyer held his legs up. I pushed him to one side, grabbed Evan's shirt and tie, and hauled him out like a drowned kitten. His thin hair streamed and water sputtered messily from his nose and mouth, but he didn't look ready to die yet. He was just settling onto the ledge of the fountain for a coughing fit when someone grabbed my right shoulder and spun me round to meet a fist.

The impact was a distant thing, after all. I hardly moved, though Dreyer must have put everything he had into it. Now he was hunched over his sore hand and glaring at me, probably working up to try again with the one he had left.

"Let it go," I told him.

"He cheated," he stated flatly.

I was the center of attention now and all of them looked one word away from beating me up for interfering with their fun. There were too many for me to influence, but it didn't seem necessary to try. Dreyer was the leader and would be the one to convince.

"So don't play with him," I suggested.

"Go to hell," he snarled back.

He looked ready to take another swing. From the stink of booze on his breath he might be just drunk enough or dumb enough to try. If so, then I'd make damn sure he lived to regret it.

"Forget it, Dreyer," someone from the rear said. "Let's get the money and go."

A few of the more practical ones broke away to count cash, but kept a wary eye open to watch any developments. Dreyer didn't move.

"*C'mon*, he's not worth the trouble."

Dreyer seemed to be having an internal debate over that point, then abruptly straightened from his near crouch. Before he could think twice about things, I caught up Evan and hustled him out of the war zone.

No one followed as we threaded through the maze of hedges. Evan had got his breath back, but still held a hand to his sore face where a beaut was forming on his left jaw.

"Thanks, buddy, I owe you one. They were really going to kill me."

"Just one of them—and you're welcome."

"Yeah, Dreyer's a real bastard. Come on back to the house, I'll buy you a drink."

He was more in need of it than I, but there was nothing better to do until Bobbi was finished. He knew the place and directed me around to a side entrance that opened into the kitchen. It was another enormous room and equipped with enough food and utensils to serve Wrigley Field during a sellout. We both winced at the bright light and bustling staff until a tubby young woman in white spotted us and came over, hands on her hips.

"Good grief, is that you, Mr. Robley?"

"What's left of him, Jannie," he shot back with a smile, and then winced at the action. "Got an ice pack?"

She sighed and shook her head at the wreckage and motioned for me to drop him in a chair next to one of the sinks. She found a towel and began to sop up his excess water. "What happened this time?"

"Well, there was this swimming contest—"

She dropped another towel over his face and rubbed briskly, his pained protests overriding his story. "Walt!" One of the white-coated waiters hustled over, grinning from ear to ear. "Go get a robe from the bathhouse storage and then try and find Miss Robley." He nodded and left, no doubt happy to be the one to pass the news along.

Evan fought his way out of the towel. "There's no need to bring Sandra into this, this is the first break she's had in a month of Sundays."

Jannie ignored him and made an ice pack with his towel and lumped it firmly against the sore side of his face. He yelped, but held it in place while she returned to direct some business on the other side of the kitchen.

"Women," he moaned. "They're all sympathy until you really need some. I get into the least little bit of trouble and they automatically think it's my fault."

I nodded and pretended to agree.

"Jannie's nice, though; a little bossy, but she's got beautiful skin tones. A little white, a touch of umber . . ." He saw that he'd lost me and made a writing motion in the air. "For painting? You know—art?"

"You're an artist?"

"One of the few genuine ones at this party."

Jannie returned with something that looked like a sheet with sleeves. "Start taking them off, Mr. Robley."

"What—here?"

"It's warm enough with the stoves," she pointed out with easy practicality.

"Warmth isn't what I'm concerned about." He indicated some of the female staffers.

"They know what a man looks like, and *you* more than most."

He was close to blushing. "This isn't fair—"

She smiled down at him. "I said the same thing to you on that so-called modeling job you gave me, so shuck 'em."

"That was art, this is . . . is . . ."

"Revenge," she concluded sweetly.

Some of the other girls gathered around in a scene disturbingly similar to the one we'd faced by the fountain. I backed away, he was strictly on his own this time.

"Perhaps you'd like some help, Mr. Robley. . . ."

"No, thanks, I know how it's done," he said, inspiring a burst of giggles. Grumbling, he started peeling off his coat. When he wrestled free of it and his shirt he grabbed up the huge robe and belted himself in before unbuttoning his pants. Jannie gathered it all together in a basket.

"What about the rest?"

"My socks aren't wet."

"I mean your—"

"They're dry, too," he insisted grimly, and sat on the chair to preclude any attempt to remove his last shred of dignity. Jannie passed the basket on to another girl with instructions to dry things out.

Walt returned, ushering in a tall young woman dressed in rich green satin. Her russet eyes swept the room and fastened on Evan, who hunched a bit lower in his robe, looking supremely miserable. She came over and regarded him with amused tolerance.

"I was told you'd had an accident," she said judicially.

"Er . . . yes, something like that." He was definitely blushing by now. "There was a roughhouse, see, and I got caught up in the middle of it, and if my friend here hadn't stepped in and saved my life . . . well . . ."

"Oh, *Evan*."

"I did *not* throw the first punch, I swear." He held up his hand, which was hidden by half a yard of sleeve. He noticed, quickly lowered it, and fastened on me as a distraction. "Sandra, I'd like to introduce you to . . . uh . . ."

"Jack Fleming," I said, rescuing him again, and we shook briefly.

"Thank you for taking care of him. You're not hurt?"

"Only a little damp, Evan took the real damage."

"But I'm fine." A few shards of ice from the towel fell out as he struggled to free his hand from the sleeve. "Evan Robley," he said to me, "soon to be famous—along with my lovely, understanding sister, of course."

"How so, famous?"

"Because a lot of artists only become famous after they're dead," she put in significantly.

They had the same coloring, sharp features, and paint-stained fingers. His sandy hair was straight, hers was curly and a deep russet like her eyes. She had a slender build, but the fragility was offset by her long, firm jaw; tough looking, but not unattractive.

"Do you want to go home?" she asked him.

"No, not at all. Jannie'll have my clothes back in two shakes. Why don't you two go on and enjoy the party?"

"I can't just leave you—"

"I'll be fine." He appealed to me. "Take her back to the party and make her have some fun. Please?"

Her head tilted to one side in challenge. Sandra wasn't the type who could be made to do anything she didn't want. She noted my hesitation with amusement and suddenly smiled in approval. Sometimes my easy-to-read face could be an asset.

"Stay out of trouble?" she told him.

"Don't I always try?"

Sandra slipped her hand under my arm and led the way out of the kitchen.

"It just keeps finding me, is all," he muttered under his breath.

I glanced back in time to see Evan begin an animated conversation with one of the maids.

"Are you here with a date, Mr. Fleming?"

"Jack. Yes, I am, and yourself?"

"Evan's my escort. He wandered off rather early. What happened this time?"

"Cra—dice game. Some of the boys didn't like the way he was throwing them."

"Not those loaded ones *again*?"

"He'll have to get new ones, he lost them in the struggle."

"The sad thing is he probably will. He never seems to learn."

"Like a drink?" I offered as a waiter approached. She nodded and I swept a glass off for her. "Does Evan sell much of his art?"

"Hardly any, his work is too different for conventional tastes, but I manage to sell some things now and then."

"Beauty, brains, and talent. Congratulations. What do you paint?"

"Anything that sells, I'm afraid."

"Isn't that good?"

"For money, I suppose it is, but it's not always good for artistic integrity."

"What do you mean?"

"Do you know anything about art?"

"I'm learning now."

She finished her glass of champagne and deposited the empty on another passing tray. "Come on, I'll give you a lesson in the basics." She took me away from the mainstream of the party into the more sparsely populated areas of the house.

"You know this place pretty well?" I asked, trying to keep track of the layout.

"Oh, yes, we're very good friends with Leighton and Reva. I've sometimes spent as much time in Leighton's studio as my own."

"I thought artists were always in competition with each other."

"To a certain extent that's true, but we also exchange ideas and critiques. Of course it usually depends on the artist. Evan and Leighton have totally different styles, so they appeal to different tastes. Now look at this one, something you could hang anywhere in the world, in almost any house."

We paused in front of a landscape of mountains with a flowing, cloudy sky. There was a lot of detail to it, the colors were pleasant to look at, and it was very similar to the rural scenes in Gordy's office.

"What do you think?" she asked.

"I'm not sure, I don't feel qualified to judge."

"Do you know what you like?"

"Yes . . ."

Her attention sharpened. "But what?"

"I don't know, maybe it seems just a little too perfect."

She took my arm again. "Let me show you some more."

We explored the open areas of most of the downstairs rooms, squeezing close to all the walls and studying enough canvas to support a small museum. Leighton Brett's style was distinctive to himself, but for some reason I couldn't get into his paintings for more than a minute or so. I couldn't imagine buying one to look at for years at a time. Sandra was delighted.

"What's this about?"

Her smile had a definite softening effect on her face. "You are one of the few people I've met who've spotted it."

"What did I spot, then?"

"Leighton's artistic manipulation."

"What's that?"

She gestured at the painting, this one of a vase of flowers. "See the colors, very bland except for this touch of red here and here, which gives it all balance. I'm not denying he has a great deal of technical skill, but it's all very carefully planned, as you said, just a little too perfect." Her attitude was more amusement than jealousy, like a teacher instructing a pupil and enjoying the interaction for its own sake.

I looked at the flowers again and knew that with or without Sandra's information I still wouldn't like it. "What do you paint?"

"The same sort of things as Leighton, only I don't get paid as much. I was lucky enough to get in on the WPA program to produce art for federal buildings, which certainly helps at rent time."

"I didn't know the WPA even had a program for artists."

"Oh yes, and it's saved more than a few lives."

"Do you paint what you like or what they tell you?"

"A bit of both. Remember what I said about artistic integrity? They don't really dictate what they want to me, but I am expected to paint something acceptable. Leighton's a great help to me there, he has a knack for knowing exactly what people expect, and then gives it to them. Whenever I think I'm going dry, I come over here for a refresher course."

"How does he feel about that?"

"He doesn't know about it," said a dark-haired man, turning around from his own station near the still life. "And since Sandra is quite tactful, he never will."

Sandra flashed a very devastating smile on him and touched his arm with an impulsive hand. "Alex! I'm so glad you came. How are you?"

His response to her obvious affection was minimal. His body

went stiff at her touch and then relaxed visibly, as though he had to consciously remember she was a friend. "I'm well enough."

He didn't look it. He held his body straight, but his clothes were loose from weight loss and the skin on his face was dull. The impression was not so much ill health as neglect. The term "walking dead" had a more meaningful application to him than to myself. His suit was expensive but unpressed, and his collar and cuffs frayed beyond saving. He noticed my assessment and a slight spark of resentment lit his dark eyes for a brief second, then went out. He didn't give a damn.

I understood why when Sandra introduced us. Alex Adrian: one of the very few who had become famous outside artistic circles. In the last ten years hardly a week went by that his work didn't appear on some major or even minor magazine. He was in demand for snob advertising, illustrative work, society portraits, you name it, his talent crossed all boundaries and had kept him at the top. But this year, in January, the work stopped, and with enough notoriety to make headlines in more places than Chicago.

We shook hands briefly to obey social convention and then he pulled back into himself, hands held in front, the fingers of the right slowly twisting his wedding band around. I was interested to note he still wore it, perhaps as silent defiance to the rumors he'd murdered his wife.

"How is your WPA work going?" he asked Sandra.

"As well as possible, I'm working on a series for a civil-service building in Rockford."

"What are you doing?"

"Mountains, flowers, and sunsets; I don't know what the building looks like so I'm assuming the workers there would be glad of a little color."

"No doubt. Has Evan sold anything lately?"

"Another nude to Mr. Danube, and too far below the asking price."

"Tell him to stop having those pre-negotiation drinks with his buyers. What about that gallery deal?"

"It fell through. I was hoping to talk with Reva about carrying some of Evan's more restrained work."

"Why doesn't he do it himself?"

"You know how it is, Alex. He just can't seem to manage; I've tried. I pushed him in the right direction tonight and he ended up in the back fountain again."

Adrian almost looked interested. "Again?"

"Jack fished him out this time. He's in the kitchen waiting for his clothes to dry."

"Perhaps I'll check up on him, if only to protect the virtue of Brett's hired help."

"The hired help are perfectly able to look after themselves," said Evan, breaking in. His hair was combed, if a little flat, and though his clothes were still damp and wrinkled, he was cheerful. "You're looking awful, Alex, you should drink more." He held up a glass as an example and drained half of it away.

"No luck with Jannie?" said Sandra wryly.

"Not with Jannie, no. What are you all talking about me for?"

"We'd exhausted the conversational possibilities of the weather," said Adrian.

"But not drying paint," Evan shot back. "Done anything lately?"

"No."

Adrian's tone was not encouraging. Sandra noticed it and changed the subject. "Evan, I saw Reva in the small drawing room—"

"That's a good trick in this crowd."

"Evan—"

He held up a placating hand. "Peace, dear baby sister, I'll take care of it in my own way."

"When?"

"On a day when Reva doesn't have hundreds of people around her, all wanting one thing or another. This isn't the right time. The day after tomorrow, maybe."

"Why so long?"

"Because if she feels tomorrow the way I plan to feel, she'll need her rest. The day after, she'll be recovered a little from the shock but still be tired and fairly vulnerable to suggestion. That's when I'll tackle her on the gallery."

"Promise?"

"Word of honor. But tonight I'm planning to make every effort to enjoy myself so that when I tell Reva what a wonderful hostess she is, she'll know I'm sincere and not merely flattering her. Now, would anyone else like a drink? No? Then I'll just help myself." He finished the rest of his glass and went off in search of more.

Sandra half started after him, but Adrian gently caught her arm. "Let him go, you can't live his life."

Sandra glared at him a moment, then her face softened. She had a lot of things to say about the subject and managed to pack it all into that one look before nodding agreement. "All right, but I am going to see he eats at least one sandwich before he starts his debauch." She went after him.

"She's his younger sister?" I asked.

Adrian continued to twist his ring. "Yes, but a good deal more responsible, so she seems older. I'm sure he'll get his work into Brett's gallery, his plan for talking to Reva was sound enough. Sometimes he's not as foolish as he appears."

"And other times?"

Adrian abruptly smiled, showing a row of large but perfect teeth. "He is exactly as he seems." The smile vanished just as abruptly as though it had never happened. "How did Evan manage to end up in the back fountain?"

I briefly recounted the crap game and fight.

"Dreyer?" he interrupted.

"You know him?"

"I've heard of him, he's not exactly polite society. I'm surprised you were able to handle him; generally the man's a maniac. It's just like Evan to try cheating him at his own game."

"He's a gambler?"

"I'm not certain. Chicago seems to specialize in his type, if you know what I mean. I wonder why he's at this party, but then a lot of other unsavories are here as well. Money and manners don't always go together."

I remembered Madison Pruitt and could see his point.

"Are you connected with the art world, Fleming?"

"Not really, my girlfriend is singing here tonight and wanted me along."

"Bobbi Smythe? You're very fortunate. I heard her, she has a lovely voice."

"I'll tell her you said so." And that's when the idea clicked in my head. "Alex, how does one go about commissioning a painting?"

"I couldn't say for other artists. For myself, I decide what I want to work on. The general rule is half payment in advance and half on completion. Why do you ask?"

"I wanted to get a special present for Bobbi, she won't take trinkets from me, but I don't think she could turn down her own portrait."

"Especially one by Alex Adrian." He wasn't boasting, but simply aware of his talent and reputation.

"Would you consider taking on a commission?"

He did at least think it over before shaking his head. "I have to say no. It's not the subject or you, I just haven't the time. I'm sorry. Perhaps you could commission Evan or Sandra, they're both very competent. Evan in particular, when you can get him to do realism. I warn you, though. Go along with Miss Smythe during the modeling sessions. Evan rather enthusiastically fits most people's cliché ideas of an artist. I think if he had no talent at all he would still be an artist, if only to exploit the popular reputation involved."

"You're certain you won't take it?"

"Very certain. Sorry."

He excused himself and moved back into the crowd. He was puzzling, because I was positive for a moment that he was going to say yes. The dullness had left his face, and even in the packed room, I'd heard his heart hammer a little faster. He'd been genuinely interested and then the walls had come up, visibly and quite sudden. I glanced around to see if anything had inspired the change. The only thing in his direct line of sight were people, none of them known to me, but then a woman moved her head and I saw Reva Stokes, smiling and playing hostess.

She caught my look and nodded, then came over, graceful, smooth, and with a warmer attitude than before now that she was certain of the success of her party. "Are you enjoying yourself, Mr. Fleming?"

"Yes, thank you."

"I saw you talking with Alex. Are you friends?"

"Just met him tonight, I take it you know him, too."

"Yes, he and Leighton are good friends. He was over here a lot before . . . before Celia died."

"Celia was his wife?"

"Yes. It was suicide, he found her in their garage. She'd shut the doors and started the car and just sat there and let it happen. What a horrible way to die."

"The papers were less than kind to him, I suppose."

"Those disgusting rags. One of the reporters all but broke into his home for an interview. Alex threw them out, and that's when they started writing those awful stories. They were clever about it, they didn't print anything they could be sued for, but the innuendo was nearly enough to ruin him. He's had to change his phone number several times because of the terrible calls, and once some kids stoned his studio and broke windows. People can be so awful."

"He did seem withdrawn."

"You can hardly blame him. He's been a complete recluse since then; I'm hoping his coming here means he's getting back to being his old self."

"Does that also mean getting back to painting?"

"I hope so. I know he hasn't done any work for months."

"He must have loved her a lot."

"Oh, yes," she agreed, absently distracted because a large man came up and put a friendly arm around her shoulders.

"How are you holding up?" he asked with good humor. He had a drink and cigarette balanced in his free hand and looked comfortably happy about the world in general. Like Reva, I knew his face from the photo in the paper.

"Just fine, Leighton," she replied. "And you?"

"I can do this for hours yet." He removed the arm from her shoulders and extended a hand at me. "Leighton Brett, guest of honor of all this madness."

"Jack Fleming."

He was larger and even more solid than the newspaper photo

implied. It only hinted at the rich, curly brown hair and had left out the laugh lines round his eyes. There was no hint of the planned calculation his paintings showed, and I wondered if Sandra had just been pulling my leg.

"Mr. Fleming is here with Bobbi Smythe, Leighton."

This garnered a broad smile. "She's doing a wonderful job in there."

"I'll be sure to tell her."

"Did you know that Alex was here tonight?" Reva asked him.

"Yes, I finally talked him into coming. It's about time he got back to normal again. He's had too much of his own company and needs to remember life goes on."

"We were just talking about Celia—"

"Not where he or anyone else could hear, I hope. You know he's just coming out of it, the last thing he needs is for all that gossip to start up again."

"It won't be repeated," I said.

"I should hope not," he rumbled, and Reva looked uncomfortable. A subject change again seemed in order.

"I had a question for you on one of your paintings—"

"Certainly, go ahead."

"The farm scene in the paper that won the award, have you painted any duplicates of it?"

"Certainly not. What do you mean, 'duplicates'?"

"I happened to see a very similar painting once before in someone's office, and I'd heard that artists sometimes make copies of their own work."

"If I want copies I do a print or an engraving. Where did you see this?"

"In a private office, three fairly big paintings. The owner got them through a decorator, but I don't know the name."

"Reva?"

She shook her head. "I don't remember selling three of that size to any one person or company, not all at once, anyway. It could be an imitator, there are a lot of them around."

"Far too many and you're being too kind, girl. Those bastards are little more than forgers, as far as I'm concerned. A man works for years to get his style, and then they just jump in and make a fortune off all my efforts. I want to see these paintings. Where are they?"

It did not strike me that Gordy would appreciate having an artist of even Brett's reputation barging around his office and asking questions. "I'm not at liberty to say, but I can ask the owner permission for you to—"

"Ask permission? Look, if someone is cheating me and the public out of my work, I want to know about it." His voice rose; apparently he was very unused to getting no for an answer.

Heads were turning and Reva had backed away, flushing beet red with embarrassment. I did what I could to keep my voice calm and even. "I can't tell you now, but I'll look into it for you, I promise."

He paused, blinked, and seemed to realize he was on the verge of making a scene. He chose to ignore it altogether. "Good, call me as soon as you know anything." His good humor returned an instant later. Reva's color evened out again, but her tone was a little forced as she drew my attention to a still life on the wall. The people around us gradually went back to their own conversations. I stuck it out and made some kind of comment or other. Brett responded well to my inexpert praise, and even indulged in some modest self-critique.

"Yes, but it's a bit old now, at least to my eyes. I've learned a lot since that one was painted. I suppose we ought to sell it off and replace it with something better."

"It looks fine to me," I said, hoping the remark didn't sound as false to him as it did to me.

Reva stepped in. "Brett always says things like that; every artist knows his next painting will be better than the last."

"And it's always true," confirmed Brett. "Have you been by the gallery yet?"

The safe and sane small talk continued until someone else claimed their attention and I could decently slip away. It was past time for me to return to the long hall and see how Bobbi was getting along.

The sound of the music was my guide, Bobbi was singing again, another slow club number that could make a statue weep. The place was as crowded as before but I managed to squeeze through and catch her eye. She gave me a discreet nod without pausing in her song of hope and heartbreak.

The crowd had backed off to create an impromptu dance floor, and couples swayed to the slow music. I was a little surprised to see Adrian among them. He didn't seem the sort to indulge in frivolity, but perhaps Sandra had talked him into it. She was one of those rare ones who could do that without seeming pushy. Her head rested contentedly against his shoulder and neither of them were in any pain.

Someone appeared abruptly at my side, Walt from the kitchen. He was looking anxiously at the dancers.

"Something wrong?" I asked.

He recognized me. "Well, yes, sort of . . . Mr. Robley . . ."

"He needs to see his sister?"

"No, sir, I think the last person he'd want to see is his sister. He mumbled something about Mr. Adrian."

It sounded ominous, but I didn't want to break in on them. All the world loves a lover and all that, and I had more than one romantic bone holding up my carcass. "He's busy, let's see if I can substitute."

Relieved, he led me out by another door to a hallway and eventually to a linen closet. Evan was at the bottom of it with blood on his face.

▲
3
▼

He moaned as the hall light hit him.

Walt said, "I was getting some more towels and found him. I thought he was just sleeping one off until I saw he was hurt. He wanted I should get Mr. Adrian to help take him home."

I knelt next to him and felt his arms and ribs. Since he didn't yell any objections, I assumed nothing was broken. "Evan? Can you tell us what happened?"

"Truck with fists," he mumbled. There was a small cut over one eye, but most of the gore was seeping gently from his nose. I borrowed one of the towels, held it to his face, and told him to tilt his head back.

"There's a bathroom just next to us," Walt offered helpfully.

We gave Evan another minute to get his breath back, then I all but carried him out. He sank gratefully onto the closed lid of the toilet and sat quietly while Walt and I cleaned off the worst of the mess. In addition to his already-bruised cheek, his left eye was swelling shut. The first real sign of life was his shocked yelp when I dabbed antiseptic on the cut.

"Who did it?" I asked.

"Dreyer—what're you trying to do, top him?" He pushed the swab of cotton away petulantly. "One of his boys must have followed me around. I've never known such a sore loser."

"I think you're the one that lost."

"Walt, be a pal and find me something for the pain."

Walt obligingly searched the medicine cabinet until Evan made it clear he wanted his painkiller in a glass with ice.

I resumed cleanup on his face. "You want to go home?"

"Yes, I think that would be a very good idea."

"What about Sandra?"

"Oh, God . . . tell her I got an unexpected date and went home early. She'll understand. I hope."

"You have a way home?"

That stumped him, so I offered him a ride, which he woozily accepted. When Walt returned I told him to keep Evan in one place while I went back to the long hall.

Bobbi was singing "Gimme a Pigfoot" to the raucous delight of the crowd, and Titus Noble's quartet was attempting an impromptu accompaniment. Sandra was still with Adrian, no longer dancing, but standing on the edge of things and clapping in time to the music. Adrian's enjoyment looked a little forced, but the hesitant smiles he gave Sandra were genuine enough. I elbowed over and passed on Evan's message to her.

"A date?" she puzzled. "Who with?"

I shrugged. "He didn't want you to worry about him, he said."

"There's a first time for everything," commented Adrian, not too helpfully.

Leaving them, I scribbled a quick note to Bobbi explaining I was driving home a drunk guest and would be back for her before the party was over. Since I couldn't interrupt her, I opted to give it to the cello player, who wasn't doing too much at the moment. I didn't trust Marza to pass it along.

Evan was anything but enthused over moving. The bruises were stiffening up, and now he insisted he'd be happy enough spending the rest of the night on the bathroom floor. When Walt offered to check with Reva about the loan of a bedroom, Evan changed his mind. One question would lead to another and eventually involve Sandra. He had no wish to listen to another sisterly lecture on the virtues of moderation and the avoidance of rough company.

Walt guided us out by a side door and would have helped us the rest of the way to my car except for Jannie's piercing shout.

The spare towels were long overdue by now. I told him to go back; Evan was a handful, but nothing I couldn't manage.

I was wrong.

The pounding on his stomach combined with that last drink ended in a predictable way. The cold night air hit Evan like a bag of cement, he went green, made a green noise in his throat, and doubled over. I was just quick enough to aim him at the flower beds before he lost it all.

"Ridiculous, isn't he?"

Adrian was in the doorway watching the show and not quite grinning.

"I've seen worse," I said truthfully. "I'm taking him home. Dreyer got to him again and he didn't want Sandra—"

"Evan never fails to be considerate of others, at least after the fact. Need some help?"

"Yeah."

When it was over we hauled Evan past the long line of cars and loaded him into the back of my Buick, where he promptly fell asleep.

"You followed?" I asked Adrian.

"Of course. Your story to Sandra didn't sound like Evan at all. When he falls in love for the evening, one generally doesn't know about it until the next afternoon. He's in no condition to give you directions now, I'll come along if you don't mind."

"Hop in."

I started it up, carefully backed out, and only remembered to turn the headlights on by correctly reading the growing alarm on Adrian's face. We rolled slowly down the drive to the distant street, and he guided us from there.

"This happen to you often?" I asked.

"If you mean taking Evan home in such a condition, yes. I've done it more than once."

"The guy that found him was looking for you at first. Sorry this had to interrupt your evening with Sandra."

"We'll be back soon enough."

"I had an interesting talk with her about Leighton Brett's art . . . do you agree with her views?"

"I'm not certain what they are."

"I thought his stuff was too perfect, she said he planned it to be that way."

"No doubt she is right. Leighton insists on a great deal of control in his life, there's no reason why his art should be different."

"Doesn't that limit creativity?"

"That depends on your approach. All good art requires control, the real skill is not letting the control itself show."

"It should look easy? Like anyone could do it?"

He glanced over once, approving. "Exactly. You end up with a thousand students going in for art. It looks easy, especially the more modern schools. That's how Evan got started. He thought that anyone could slop paint over a canvas and call it art, but he surprised himself and a few other people. He's one of the few with a true talent for the expression of an idea as well as the work."

"But what about Brett's control?"

"He paints what the public wants to see and he does it so well. Not many of them notice what's missing."

"What's that?"

"Leighton Brett."

"Yeah?"

"Art is often a process of self-revelation, but he's a careful and private man, and his work reveals nothing of what is within him. He paints what's popular and saleable and enjoys the honors involved, such as they are. All you'll know about him from his paintings a hundred years from now was that he was a competent draftsman with a streak of bogus sentiment."

"What will people know about you a hundred years from now?"

"Probably the same thing, but without the sentiment."

"I doubt that."

"Why?"

"I've seen your work—nothing bogus there."

He looked at me sidewise. I'd meant it to be a compliment; he decided to take it as such. "Are you an artist as well?"

I hesitated, considering his past associations with reporters. "I write a little, so I can understand the creative process from that angle."

"What do you write?"

Nothing so far, but you don't say that to people. I decided on the truth and if he didn't like it, too bad. "I used to be a journalist, a paper in New York, but I had to get out."

"Had to?" he asked after a long pause. "Why?"

"I didn't like what it was turning me into so I stopped and became something else. I'm free-lance now."

His voice would freeze fire. "And is this an interview?"

"No. We're just two guys driving another home and having a talk about art."

I don't think he took it at face value, but then he had no real reason to trust me. Except for his terse directions, conversation lagged, but he wasn't ready to bolt from the car yet.

We ended up in a lower-class neighborhood of tired brick buildings, cheap rent being the only obvious asset of the area. We dragged Evan from the car and got him up the steps of his house. Adrian struggled with the keys while I kept us more or less vertical.

Inside the narrow entry hall were the usual doors and stairs, which we went up, or tried to; Evan was so far gone as to be a danger to our collective balance. I had Adrian stand back, then hoisted Evan onto my shoulder in a fireman's carry.

"The strength of youth," he said, and led the way up to the second floor and opened the door of the Robleys' flat.

The front room was obviously a work area, its length running along one wall to take advantage of the north-facing windows. Two large easels were set up, one with a light cloth covering a work in progress, the other with its colorful canvas on display. The place was stuffy with the smell of linseed oil and harsh turpentine. The furnishings were sparse and unpretentious: some simple chairs and a table with a lumpy bronze sculpture as its centerpiece. A few unframed paintings clung to the walls, mixed in with a family photo or two. One of them was of two young men grinning like devils, hamming it up at some kind of carnival. A slender girl stood between them and their arms were around her. It was Sandra, a young teen just starting to bloom into a woman. One of the men was Evan, who hadn't changed much in looks or attitude. The other was Adrian, who had. A lot of years and life had come between the carefree face in the photo and the solitary, saturnine man who stood next to me.

Adrian turned on the lights and pointed me toward the back, where I found Evan's bedroom. I eased him onto the bed and threw a quilt over him. I was just debating whether to remove his shoes when I heard an oddly familiar slap-and-grunt combination and hurried out to investigate.

Adrian was doubled over, holding his stomach. A man in a cheap, gaudy suit stood just inside the front door and had apparently just walked in and punched him. A second, much larger man bulled his way past, grabbed Adrian's elbows from behind and hauled him upright with a sharp jerk. Cheap Suit laughed and landed another fist before he noticed my presence.

I grabbed the larger man from behind in his turn and pried his arms free. Adrian all but hit the floor, still trying to get his lost breath back. The big one shook an arm loose and swung it backhanded at my face. A couple of months earlier I'd have been flattened, but now I was just annoyed. I was about to let him know just how annoyed when the suit jumped in between us waving a knife under my nose.

He was grinning because he knew he had me cold, a wild-eyed maniac with bad skin and cartoon eyebrows. I released my hold on his friend. They were moving slowly now, but only because I was moving that much faster. His mouth dropped open in sluggish shock when I plucked the knife out of his hand and snapped the blade and handle in two like a dry twig. By the time he started to recover, Adrian grabbed both his shoulders and spun him around to pay his own respects.

The big one tried hitting me again. He was a solid piece of muscle and had had some sparring experience. His punches were short and controlled but I wouldn't let him get close enough to connect. This put him into a bad temper, but I wasn't feeling too kindly about things, either. I stepped into his right, trapped his arm under my own, and much to his surprise wrestled him against a handy wall, thumping his head for good measure. When we locked eyes I went in there as well, feeling righteous satisfaction when his expression went blank.

"Fall on the floor and stay there," I told him, and stepped

back out of the way. He landed hard, like a tree trunk, without putting his arms out to cushion the impact.

Adrian was too busy to notice. I'd gotten peripheral glimpses of his fight, but nothing really clear. Now it was obvious he had one hell of a temper and had just lost it. He held the man up by his loud necktie and was systematically hitting his face and gut with hard, vicious punches. His teeth were bared in a parody of a smile, and breath hissed between them each time he connected. He backed the man up to a wall, then caught his throat and started squeezing to kill.

I had to step in then or end up with a pop-eyed corpse. Adrian ignored hearing his name, but I managed to work his hands loose without breaking anything and pulled him away. The suit, considerably rumpled, sank to the floor, too battered to even moan.

Adrian suddenly became aware of things and shook me off with a muted growl. He glared at the man, puffing from the exertion, his lips peeled back wolflike, as if he'd welcome an excuse to start over again. He glanced at me, his eyes bright. The barriers were down for a moment and I wasn't sure I liked what they'd been hiding.

"Who are they?" I asked.

He checked both faces carefully, contemptuously. "Damned if I know. Probably more of Evan's friends."

"Dreyer again?"

"Perhaps."

I stooped and felt around for Cheap Suit's wallet. The Illinois license identified him as Francis Koller. He was carrying nearly eight hundred dollars, which I showed to Adrian in passing. Adrian searched the pockets of the other man.

"His name's Toumey. What's the matter with him? He looks like he's in a trance."

"Glass jaw," I said, and shoved Koller's wallet back in his pocket. He didn't look in any condition to remember his own name, much less answer questions, so I left him and knelt over Toumey, tapping his mug a few times for effect. "Hey, come out of it."

It worked faster than I expected. His eyes lost their fixed

stare and got wider. He made an abortive attempt to get up,
except I got a grip on one shoulder and leaned a knee into his
stomach. My fingers were very strong; he winced and tried to
writhe away, but Adrian was on his other side and held him
down as well.

"Okay, Toumey, you tell us all about it," I instructed.

He went slack and staring again.

"Why did you come here?"

"Shake 'im up."

"Who?"

"Robley."

"Why?"

"Owes money."

"Give me a name."

"Dimmy Wallace."

I looked at Adrian. He shook his head. "Who's Dimmy
Wallace?"

"*Shut up, Toumey.*" This from Koller, who was still flat on
his back and trying to talk through battered lips.

"He must be the brains of the outfit," I commented to
Adrian. "Toumey, you stay right where you are until I say
otherwise, got it?" Toumey nodded, his eyes glazed. Adrian
had begun to notice something odd going on, but if necessary
I could fix that, too. We switched to Koller. He was just
starting to roll over to get to his feet so we each slammed him
flat again, and none too gently.

"Dimmy Wallace," said Adrian. "Talk."

He told Adrian to go somewhere and do something. I
grabbed Koller's chin and forced him to look up at me. "Think
about it, Francis, it's two to one now and you're already
bleeding on the canvas. You want I should let my friend here
finish the job he started on you?"

"Don't call me Francis," he muttered, but contact was
established and he was under my influence for the moment.

"Who's Wallace?"

"My boss, best in the city."

"What does he do?"

"Big man, does it all."

"Gambling?"

"The works."

"A mob?"

"The biggest, the best there is."

"One can't fault him for his loyalty," Adrian remarked. "So Evan owes money to Dimmy Wallace, the one mobster in Chicago who hasn't made the papers yet."

"To judge from his hired help, I doubt he ever will. My guess is these saps don't even know what Evan looks like."

"You mean they mistook me for . . . ?" his lips thinned with disgust. "Now *that* is adding insult to injury. What do we do with them?"

"Kick 'em down the stairs?" I suggested.

He considered it. "What about informing the police?"

It was a little surprising that he would want to drag them in, especially if he still had a cloud over him because of his wife's death. To me, the cops meant charges, arrests, court appearances. Daytime stuff. "Hardly seems worth the trouble," I said, hoping I wouldn't have to talk him into it.

"Perhaps you're right. Let's throw them out."

"Hey!" was all Koller had time to say before we hauled him through the door and downstairs. I made sure he was shaken up, but not seriously hurt when we finally dropped him in the gutter outside. He started up with the obscenities again along with dire threats against the Robleys and everyone that knew them. While Adrian watched from the doorway I picked Koller up by his necktie and pushed him backward over a handy car hood.

"You got a bad mouth on you, boy, so shut it before you lose it. Go back to your roach hole and tell your boss to use the phone the next time he wants to collect on a bill. You or Toumey show up here again and—"

I didn't finish the threat, it was unnecessary. Koller saw exactly what he never wanted to see in my eyes. I gave him just enough to scare him, then let him go. He stumbled once, regained his footing, and ran down the block like hell was after him. He never looked back.

Adrian's expression was closed and watchful again. "I wish I had your way with people."

I shrugged. "Let's get the other one."

Toumey was more quiescent than his partner, content to be led to the exit and shoved out, again with the instructions never to return. We got back to the flat and checked on Evan, who had slept through the party.

Adrian stripped away the quilt, picked up a bedside carafe, and poured what was left of the contents on Evan's face. What all the roughhouse and noise failed to do a half cup of water accomplished: Evan shot awake, flailing and spitting.

"You'll drown me!" he wailed.

"Not unless I strangle you first. Wake up." Adrian went to the bathroom off the hall and brought back a towel for him.

Evan vaguely blotted at the water, confused and muttering. "First there's Dreyer, then Sandra, then Dreyer, and then you. What's the matter with everyone tonight?"

"We've all had to deal with you. Who's Dimmy Wallace?"

"Who?" he said, a little too innocently.

"Two of his people were just here," I informed him. "And we both took a beating that was meant for you, so you owe us."

"What?"

I repeated the story until he said he understood things, but his comprehension might also have had something to do with Adrian refilling the carafe.

"All right," he grumbled, "but Sandra won't like me showing the dirty laundry."

"That's never bothered you before," Adrian pointed out.

Evan snarled blearily at him. "In your ear."

The carafe began to tilt.

"I didn't mean it! Dimmy's my bookie, sort of."

"We're listening."

"That's it—really. He gave me some credit on my losses, said he'd wait until I sold something. Well, I sold something, but then he said I owed him interest as well. I told him to wait until I sell another painting, but he's not the patient kind—"

"And the longer it takes to pay, the more your interest increases?" I put in.

"Exactly."

"You've paid the original debt, though?"

"And then some."

I had a deep and very sincere stab of sympathy for Sandra.

Adrian was simply exasperated but willing to take action. "Get your toothbrush, Evan. Sandra's as well."

"Huh?"

"I'm not leaving her alone in this house while people like that are after you."

"But *I'm* here!"

"As I said, she's not going to be left alone."

Maybe I could have assured him the toughs wouldn't be back, but someone like Dimmy Wallace would have others to take their place. "Okay, you guys pack the toothbrushes, I'll drive."

About ten minutes later we were in the car, making a circle back toward Leighton Brett's neighborhood, but not quite. The mirror was clean, no one had followed us.

Adrian directed me to a less pretentious area of quiet houses with demure picket fences and regular streetlights. His home was a long one-storied structure, with a closed garage on one side. On the paving in front of it was an oil stain marking the spot where his car usually stood. Somehow I wasn't too surprised he no longer used the garage for its original purpose.

Evan was installed in a long-unused guest room and went thankfully back to sleep with a soft groan. Adrian threw a blanket on him and shut off the lights.

"He might be disoriented when he wakes up," I cautioned.

"It won't be a new experience for him."

I followed him into the kitchen. Perhaps it had been a bright place once; cheery little feminine knickknacks decorated the walls and cupboards. Now they were dull with dust, and the once-fluffy white curtains hung limp and dejected. The usual litter of inexpert cooking and casual cleanup cluttered the counters, and a plate with its dried scraps rested on the table where Adrian had eaten the latest in a series of solitary meals.

He rummaged around in some half-opened parcels on the table and brought out a box of headache powders. He mixed a double dose in a glass of water and drank it straight down. "Need any?" he offered.

"No, thanks."

He edged the glass in with a dozen others by the sink. The sad atmosphere of the house was uncomfortable. It seemed to ooze from the walls, or more likely from Adrian. Either from his wife's death or by his natural temperament, he'd turned everything inward, and though too polite to obviously show it, he did not like having a stranger in his home, especially an observant ex-journalist.

When we got back to the party his posture relaxed slightly. He'd gone from being on guard to something else I couldn't quite read, and was twisting his wedding ring around again.

"Thank you," he murmured. "I'll find Sandra and tell her what happened."

"Anytime," I said to his departing back as he disappeared into the crowd.

Bobbi was still in the big hall, but taking a break, or trying to. I could hardly see her for all the men grouped around, offering her enough drinks for a chorus line. One of them was Titus. He was close to Bobbi but facing outward, and doing a reasonable protection job by keeping the worst of the interlopers at bay. I squeezed my way to the center to relieve him. Without a word he took her hand and gave it to me, an exaggerated gesture, but necessary considering the tipsy state of most of the men. A few backed off to give us room, and we escaped into the garden again.

She drew a deep breath and laughed a little. "Thought I was going to smother. Titus tries his best, but he's not as tall as you."

"Things did look a little crowded."

"Marza says they're like a pack of dogs following a—" She suddenly blushed. "Never mind, I had one glass of champagne and it's making me rude."

"You get my note?"

"Yes, who'd you take home?"

"Some artist I met here. He had a little too much party so we took him to Alex Adrian's house—"

"*The* Alex Adrian?"

"Absolutely. I met him tonight."

"I had no idea he was here. What's he like?"

"Distant. The sort of smoldering type women go crazy for, except in his case I think the fire's gone out."

"Must be because of his wife."

"What do you know about it?"

"That she committed suicide, maybe, or was murdered, maybe. You met him. What do you think?"

"The jury's still out for me. Are you on a break or is the party over yet?"

"I'm on a break. My contract expires at one A.M., and then you can take me home and put me to bed."

"With great pleasure, but I thought—"

"You thought right. I *am* tired, so I'm very glad I decided to seduce you earlier. Do you mind just tucking me in?"

I pulled her close and let her know exactly how I felt on that subject.

Rather than let her out of my sight again, I sat in the hall, gritting my teeth through the string quartet pieces until I could take her home. It was twenty minutes to quitting time when Sandra Robley drifted in, spotted me, and came over.

"Thank you for helping Evan," she said as I stood.

"You're welcome."

"Would *you* please tell me what happened?"

"Alex clam up on you?"

"It's his specialty. He said there was some trouble, but won't tell me what kind or why it means Evan and I have to stay at his house for the night."

"He thought it might be safer." I briefly outlined what had happened at her flat. "We didn't break anything, but he wasn't about to leave you and Evan alone with those goons on the loose. You know about Dimmy Wallace?"

"Only that Evan owes him money."

I had an idea or two on how to help them, but decided to wait before committing myself.

"It's unbelievable that these people think they can just walk in—and neither of you thought to call the police?"

"Well, I—"

She made a dismissive gesture. "At least I know how Alex's knuckles got scraped. Honestly, sometimes he can be so infuriating. You as well. I'm grateful about Evan, but should it happen again, just tell me the truth, no more stories on last-minute dates."

I raised three fingers. "Scout's honor, ma'am."

She melted a little and flashed a muted version of her smile. "Thank you. Now I'm going to talk to Alex about his overprotective attitude."

It must not have been a long lecture, for about ten minutes later they both turned up again. Sandra was on his arm and he almost looked relaxed as they listened to the music.

"That's good to see." Reva Stokes appeared next to me, watching them with contentment. "No, please don't get up, I'm just passing by and wanted to check on things."

"They're special to you?"

"Very special friends. When Celia died we thought Alex might do the same thing, but tonight he seems to be coming out of it. I'm glad Sandra's there for him."

"Sandra seems pretty glad about it as well. I wish her luck."

"With a brother like Evan, she'll need it. I haven't seen him for a while, I hope he's—"

"Alex and I took him home earlier. He was tired."

She made a wry face. "Is that what you call it?"

"When in polite society, yes. Thank you for having me along, it's meant a lot to Bobbi."

"You're welcome. Are you in the entertainment business yourself?"

"In a way. I'm a writer."

"What do you write?"

Good question. I gave her a song and dance about a novel I'd started in high school and she lost interest quickly enough. It's probably the reason I never finished the thing and went into journalism instead.

One o'clock finally came and Bobbi launched into one last song, its theme concerned with saying good night and good-bye. A few of the more sober guests took the hint and drifted out, and Reva vanished to see them on their way. Bobbi finished and took her bows, and I felt free to intrude on the stage area before various young swains flooded her with offers of a ride home.

"Fleming."

It was Adrian. Sandra was busy for the moment talking with a trio of gaunt-looking women dressed in black velvet.

"Everything okay? I had to tell Sandra about—"

"Yes, that's all fine now. I wanted to clear some business up with you . . . about that portrait commission."

He had my full attention. "Yeah, what'd you want to clear?"

Adrian didn't quite meet my eye, but it seemed more from diffidence than anything shifty. He was like a man unsure of the thickness of ice under his feet. "Did you still want to engage me for the commission?"

"Yes, certainly, but—"

"Do you think you can afford it?"

I couldn't fault him for his honesty—or at least bluntness. "How much?" He named a figure I could live with and I told him so. "Is it a deal?"

He didn't answer right away, apparently still testing the ice within him. "Yes . . . I think so. The usual procedure is half down and half on delivery."

"Fine. I can get it for you tomorrow, if that's okay."

"One thing, Fleming. I—I'm not sure I can do it. . . . If I find I cannot, I'll return the money."

I nodded. "Fair enough. And if you can?"

"Then you get your portrait and I get the balance, of course."

"Deal." I held out my hand. He didn't seem to understand what it was there for at first, then hesitantly shook it. "What made you change your mind?"

From his wallet he gave me a business card with his name and number. "Call me sometime tomorrow and we'll work out a schedule for the sittings. Good night." He turned and went back to Sandra.

Bobbi broke off her chatting with Titus and came over. "What was that all about? Who was—"

I slipped an arm around her. "*The* Alex Adrian, and that was about my Christmas present to you."

"I see what you mean about smoldering—what Christmas present?"

"Well, it might take that long for the paint to dry."

"Jack—"

"You said you didn't want diamonds, but what about your portrait done by—"

She gave out a soft shriek of pure delight and threw her arms around me in a stranglehold.

4

IT WAS NEARLY two-thirty by the time I'd dropped off Marza and Madison, saw Bobbi safe into her hotel apartment, and said good-bye. I had hours yet before dawn and these were always the hardest to fill. Bobbi invited me to stay, but she was exhausted, so I left her to her well-earned sleep.

The streets were fairly empty: only the odd carload of party goers hooting past and an occasional lonely figure wrapped against the night and out on God knows what business. I was driving north again and for the second time that week parked close to the Nightcrawler Club and walked up the steps past the big doorman. He nodded once at me, perhaps because someone had clued him in on Gordy's preferential treatment. It was his version of a polite greeting.

There was a new singer working with the band, a pretty brunette with a feisty manner. Whoever did Gordy's booking knew talent. I passed by the club and went through to the casino without trouble. The games were still going strong and would continue until either the money or the night ran out. I recognized a slab-faced blackjack dealer and sat at his table for a hand or three.

His mug was immobile, but he couldn't control his heartbeat, which I was able to hear well enough. It thumped just a little faster whenever he got a good hand. I didn't consider my listening in on his reactions to be cheating. This was just using my unnatural abilities to help ease the odds in my favor. Not all the cards were good, but when I left the table I was a sweet two hundred ahead. It'd make a nice Christmas present for my folks when the time came.

The man in the money cage said Gordy was in his office, maybe. I didn't bother to ask for an escort through the back door of the casino into the halls beyond, but one of the boys followed—just to make sure I didn't get lost, he told me.

"You gotta 'pointment?" he asked, eyeing the lines of my suit for hidden weapons. He wasn't sure if I required a frisk or not, my level of importance to his boss had yet to be established.

"Didn't know I needed one just to visit."

He looked vaguely familiar and I wondered if he'd been one of the boys who put a knife into Escott last month. I was about to ask, but the office door opened and Gordy told him to get lost. It was just as well.

"What's up?" He motioned me in and I took my usual chair.

"Nothing much, had a question or two."

"Maybe I'll answer." He sat behind his desk this time and I studied the rural landscape behind him. It certainly looked like Leighton Brett's work to my uneducated eye.

"Know anyone named Dimmy Wallace?" I asked.

"Small-time bookie and loan shark."

"Doesn't sound like much."

"He isn't. Why you want to know?"

"He's squeezing a friend of mine dry with interest on a debt he's already paid."

"It's a tough world."

"You know where I can find him?"

"I might. Who's your friend?"

"Some artist, not much sense and less money, but likable."

"Gambler?"

"Yeah. He's losing money he doesn't have."

"Name?"

"Evan Robley."

Gordy socked the name away into his memory, that much passed over his deadpan face. "You won't have to find Dimmy, I'll get the word out."

"What'll you do?"

"Tell Dimmy he's screwing 'round with a friend of mine and to lay off. I'll let some others know Robley's a bad credit risk, make it harder for him to place a bet in this town. I don't need my own bookies stretching themselves on a mark with no bucks. They got enough troubles as it is."

"Thanks, Gordy, I didn't expect you to—"

"'S nothing. How's Bobbi doin'?"

"Just beautiful, finished a job tonight at a swank home by the yacht basin. Marza did the piano and they had a string quartet for in between sets."

"Marza, huh? That broad's like sandpaper on a cut."

"I know what you mean. The guest of honor was this big-time artist, I think he may have done the paintings you have here."

Gordy's eyes traveled the walls automatically. "That'd be something, wouldn't it?"

"He doesn't remember doing them, though. I sort of promised I'd see if he had or not."

He lifted a hand. "Feel free."

I did. None of them had Brett's distinctive signature. I turned the woodscape over and just saw the name of the framers. "Did you get them from a gallery?"

"The decorator's. They had a stack of these in a bin and I picked what I liked best."

"An oil like this was in a bin?" Even I could see some work had gone into it.

"That's what I wondered, but the lady there said people pick art to go with the color of their sofa. You figure it."

"It's too screwy to figure, I'll pass." But it did sound pathetic and I could visualize hundreds of would-be Rembrandts daubing away to produce acres of mediocre canvas for the public just to make their rent payment. The difference in Gordy's case was the quality of the work. These were something I could live with, and I hadn't liked the stuff in Leighton Brett's home.

"What decorators?"

"Place downtown, they're in the book."

It was another swank place, but then between the club and casino Gordy could afford it. At this hour of the morning it was very firmly closed, not that that stopped me. I had nothing better to do. Going to an all-night movie or tiptoeing around the house so as not to wake Escott had no appeal at the moment. I slipped inside the street door of the decorator's and scented the air.

No watchman, but it wasn't exactly a bank. The average thief isn't interested in pieces of fabric or carpet patterns, and the chances of cash on the premises were slim. I prowled through pseudo–living rooms, looked at pictures on display, and found the bin of oil paintings Gordy mentioned. Several bins, in fact: unframed canvases of all sizes, with every kind of art style from every period, they were determined to please everyone. A few were signed, but most were anonymous, which bothered me. Either the artists were too modest or not proud enough. One or two were interesting, but I didn't find any that resembled Brett's style.

The office was locked, which was no problem; I just slipped inside. The desk drawers were also locked. Problem. Breaking the drawers open wouldn't be very nice and I didn't have Escott's talent for undetectable burglary. One of these nights I'd have to ask him for a few basic lessons. My curiosity wasn't that urgent, though, and neither was Brett's, as far as I was concerned. He could have the name of the place and run his own investigation.

Escott wasn't home when I woke up the next night, but he'd read my note and gotten the requested cash from his hidden safe. Because of the big crash, neither of us trusted banks, and because of his association with me, we'd both ended up with a parcel of money that needed a cache. His solution was to purchase an extremely solid safe and then carefully hide it.

He had a passion for secret panels, hidden doors, and similar camouflage, and the skill to indulge himself. The original basement steps were made of wood, hardly more than a scaffold running along the wall. He thought they were too rickety for regular use and had a contractor come in and build something considerably more solid. He was careful to choose bricks that matched those on the outside of his house and then went to some effort to age them so that they would look like part of the original construction. He supervised the whole thing and even tried his hand at bricklaying, then paid off the workmen before they had finished the job.

He lugged the safe into the dead space under the stairs and started building up the courses. By the time he was finished, the safe was sealed in for the life of the house, but by pushing on a certain brick, four square feet of a solid-looking wall pivoted open, giving one complete access to the combination lock and door. He piled a few pieces of old furniture around the stairs to complete the effect of a derelict area. It was a neat job and he was proud of it.

I had the combination, but usually had him play teller whenever I needed money because he was particular about preserving the dust around the opening. When I checked, there was no evidence he'd touched the area in months, but the cash was in an envelope on the table next to my earth-lined cot. I switched the money to my wallet, picked out some clothes, and went upstairs to call Adrian.

Sandra answered.

"I thought you might be home by now," I said after identifying myself.

She had an unmistakable smile in her voice, which was very interesting. "No, Adrian insisted we stay a little longer, just in case. I don't mind."

The way she was looking at Adrian last night certainly supported that statement. I told her I was dropping by in an hour and to let Adrian know about it. She said yes, hung up, and then I called Bobbi.

"Want to meet the man who's going to immortalize you?"

"I've only been waiting all day. No offense," she added.

"None taken, I'll be right by."

My last call was to Leighton Brett, and I left the name of Gordy's decorator with one of the maids. From there on he was on his own.

Bobbi was dressed in a beautiful cream-colored suit with touches of brown velvet on the lapels and wrists. The hemline was low enough to be in fashion, but high enough to maintain a man's interest; the neckline deep, but not scandalous. She looked perfect, and all I wanted to do when I saw her was rip off the wrappings and carry her to the nearest couch for some serious fooling around. I settled for a kiss of greeting for the moment and escorted her down to my car.

We were both full of talk, the kind of happy nonsense that all lovers indulge in. She was still flying high from her job last night and her agent was arranging yet another radio spot.

"Will it be national again?" I asked.

"I don't know yet, but I've got that local broadcast next Saturday. Will you come to the studio and watch?"

"Just try and stop me. Need a ride there?"

"Of course."

"Marza, too?" This was less enthusiastically offered.

"Not this time, she has a job elsewhere that night."

"Gee, that's too bad."

"Admit it, Jack, you're ready to turn handsprings."

"Not really, I'd have to stop the car first."

I parked in Adrian's drive just behind his black coupe and opened Bobbi's door. "You nervous?"

"A little. I can't help but wonder about his wife."

The thought had occurred to me as well, but there wasn't much I could do about the situation. We walked up to the front door, which was immediately opened by Sandra. She'd exchanged her party clothes for some wide-legged slacks and a bright scarf to keep her curly hair in place. She had a dust cloth in one hand, a spotted apron around her slim waist, and looked very domestic except for the impishness in her eyes. She let us in and I did introductions.

"You're just in time for fresh coffee." She led the way to the kitchen, which had changed considerably since last night. The curtains were clean and the clutter cleared. You could actually sit at the table and see what it looked like. "It's funny, but it's so much easier to clean someone else's place than your own. Cream and sugar?"

Bobbi had a cup, I politely begged off. "I hope this wasn't too disruptive for you."

"What? Getting yanked out of my own home in fear for my life? Whatever gave you that idea?"

I thought of telling her it was all right to go back, but decided it would be best to let Evan know first. He may have had a rough time from Sandra today about his shortcomings and would be glad for some good news to give her.

"It hasn't been so bad, and I think the company's been good for Alex, but I'll want to go back soon."

"Too much housework?" asked Bobbi.

"Not enough paint. I never feel good about myself unless I paint a little each day, and cleaning isn't very spiritually fulfilling, if you know what I mean."

Bobbi commiserated, then I asked about Adrian.

"He's in his studio. He's been getting things ready since he got up this morning. I'm so happy to see him starting work again. This is what he's needed for so long."

"I should think the magazines would still want his art."

"They do, but since the . . . since his wife died he's refused their commissions. He'd shut himself away for so long we were afraid he'd never come out. I hope this will help him to do it."

"So do we. How's Evan doing?"

"He's got some awful bruises, but seems to feel all right. He's in the studio helping Alex. The place has been shut tight since January so there was some cleaning to do."

"If we've come too soon—"

"Not at all. Alex said this was the business meeting and he'll want to set up a schedule for the sittings with Miss Smythe. I'll take you through now."

The studio was just off the kitchen, a very large room seamlessly added onto the original lines of the house. A bank of high windows ran along its north wall to catch the light. They were open even now but covered with long white curtains that moved with the night breeze like lazy ghosts.

Except for an overstuffed couch and chair in the center, all the furnishings were geared toward Adrian's work. On one end were two slanted drawing tables, one with a light arranged beneath it to shine up through its translucent top. Other, more obscure equipment lined the walls and a huge network of shelving held his supplies and finished work. In the center of the room was his easel, heavier and more complicated than the ones the Robleys owned. I felt like an intruder in a sorcerer's cave.

"Jack!" Evan looked up from his beer and hobbled over. His eye was still swollen shut and the area around it was gorgeously colored. "Recovered from last night, eh? Boy, was that a party or what?"

"Bobbi, this is Mr. Robley . . ."

He took her hand and tenderly kissed the back of it. "Evan to you, my sweet, and I'm your slave for life."

"Which is hardly an asset," said Adrian, stepping forward. "I'm Alex Adrian, Miss Smythe. I enjoyed your singing at the party very much." He neatly slipped her hand away from Evan and shook it, then mine. "Please come in." He gestured at the sofa and pulled up an old chair for himself. He looked different from last night; less formal and guarded. His manner with Bobbi hinted at the possibility of some considerable personal charm.

Sandra disappeared and Evan puttered in the background of the studio while we worked out the less artistic details of creation. There was some discussion on the size of canvas to be used and how to pose Bobbi.

"I'm not sure," she confessed. "You're the expert. Have you a recommendation?"

"Yes," Evan said promptly.

"Be decent for once," Adrian warned.

"What I recommend is a neoclassic version of Goya's *Maja Desnuda* with less surrounding background."

"I told you to be decent."

"Well, she can leave her clothes *on*, of course! It's the *pose* I'm talking about—that air of sensual relaxation. If you don't pick up on that, Alex, I swear I'll come in and paint it myself."

"You may try."

"*What* kind of pose?" asked Bobbi, carefully separating the words.

Adrian smiled. "Evan is suggesting I do a full-length portrait of you reclining on pillows. The choice of what to wear or not wear is entirely up to you, though."

"Oh, good," she said in mock relief.

The next point to work out were the sittings, something I'd have to miss since they'd be during the day for the sunlight. Evan's input had its effect and Bobbi asked if it would be all right if she could bring a friend along to watch. Adrian had no illusions about her wish for a chaperon, but then he had no objections, either.

"Three sittings, then," he announced. "An hour or so each should take care of it."

"But shouldn't it take much longer? I thought these things went on for weeks."

Evan broke in again. "Not with an expert like Alex and his style of work. What you're paying for is all the training he soaked up in the fancy French art institute he went to."

"And you should go there, Evan."

"There's a difference between an institute and an institution, no, thank you. Besides, I don't speak French."

I gave Adrian his half payment in an envelope. He seemed to approve of the straight cash and made out a receipt, which concluded the business meeting.

"If you've the time," he said, "I can make a preliminary sketch right now, just to block in the general form."

Bobbi glanced at me. I shrugged and nodded. Adrian had me move off the couch, produced a pillow, and told Bobbi to get comfortable. She suppressed a grin and relaxed back on the pillow. Adrian stood off a few feet, returned, and adjusted the position of her arm and backed off again.

"There's some strain on the line of the neck," Evan observed.

Adrian took the suggestion and tilted Bobbi's head a little. When he was satisfied he pulled one of the drawing tables from the wall and went to the storage shelves for a huge sheet of clean paper and a stick of charcoal. He made a half dozen sweeping lines and added a few precise strokes for details.

His face was totally different now that he was focused on the work. I saw serenity as well as concentration. Evan and I no longer existed for him; all that was important was his eye, his hand, and the model.

He reached a stopping point and had Bobbi come over for a look. Evan and I crowded in as well. The sofa had turned into a chaise lounge covered in plump pillows, but not so much that they overwhelmed Bobbi's reclining figure. She was languid but with an alertness in her eyes that seemed to dare the viewer

to come closer. Her clothes were more suggestive of sweeping
robes than the smart suit she wore, but anything else would
have been inappropriate for the mood he was setting up.

"Is that what you see?" she asked.

"On a good day, yes. Will it do?"

"Absolutely. If this is the sketch, I can't wait to see the
finished painting. This is like magic."

"Evan, I've some prepared canvas somewhere. . . ."

"Yeah, I put them . . . I'll get them." He rooted around
and produced several sterile white canvases, already stretched
and nailed over wood frames. Adrian chose the largest and put
it on the massive easel.

I thought he'd repeat the sketch on the canvas, but instead he
took a pin to the paper and punched tiny holes through it along
all the major lines.

"What's he doing?" I whispered to Evan.

"It's how he transfers the sketch," he whispered back.
"When he's got enough holes in it, he'll position the drawing
where he wants on the canvas, then hit at it with a small bag of
charcoal dust. The holes allow the dust to leave a guide mark
for him to follow."

"Why not just draw on the canvas?"

"Too hard to clean off if you should change your mind about
something."

The sketch drifted to the floor as he shifted his attention to
the canvas, and I could see now how he was able to keep up
with the demands the magazines had put on him. Only a few
more minutes passed and he added in all the necessary details.
Bobbi's face appeared out of the blankness, taking on expression and life.

He stood back again, studying it with a critical eye, but was
apparently satisfied. "That will do for tonight, tomorrow I'll
see to the underpainting, and you can come by the day after for
the first sitting."

"I still can't get over the speed," she said.

Adrian found a rag and scrubbed at the charcoal dust
clinging to his fingers. "Most of the time involved has to do
with allowing the paint to dry—at least that's how it is for the

way I work. All I ask is that after the final varnish dries you take it to a decent framer."

"We wouldn't do anything less."

Bobbi was looking with interest at some of the painted canvases stacked in slots and asked to see them, and Adrian obliged. Evan said he wanted another beer and invited me for one as well. I again turned down the offered drink, but tagged along to the kitchen.

"I've got some good news for you," I said as he searched the icebox. "I talked to a friend of mine and he's telling Dimmy to lay off on the interest payments."

He stopped cold. "Say that again."

I repeated it.

"Who's your friend?" he asked with amiable suspicion.

"Someone with an interest in art. He knows Dimmy and said he'd fix it. You and Sandra can probably go back home now."

"Honestly?"

"True blue."

"How in the world did you do it?"

"Well . . ."

"Never mind. Perhaps it's better I don't ask, you shouldn't question miracles, they're too few and far between." He popped the cap from a brown bottle. "This is great, really. I don't know what to say—except thanks—and that I don't plan to go home just yet."

"Yeah?"

He glanced around to see if anyone was in earshot and lowered his voice. "It's Sandra. You see, she's, well . . . it's her and Alex. You know . . . last night." He took a swig off the beer. "I was a bit out of things, but not that far out. Maybe I'm supposed to get upset since she's my sister, but she's a big girl now and—"

"Why should you stand in the way of romance?"

"Exactly! To tell the truth, I'd like to see her safely married or whatever to whoever—or is it whomever? Anyway, having Alex for a brother-in-law can't be much worse than having him for a friend, and she could do worse herself. Besides, it would get her out of *my* hair, that awful little walk-up we live in, and into *his* hair and a very cozy house, which is just what she needs."

"I hope it works out for you."

"Same here, so I won't come out with the glad news for a while yet, and I'm going to be fairly well oiled or at least look like I am before I turn in tonight to give them plenty of opportunity for more innocent sinning."

"Very considerate, but if you don't mind a personal question—"

"You've saved my life, so feel free."

"I was wondering about his late wife."

"Oh. That." His face fell. "What d'ya want to know?"

"Why did she kill herself?"

"Oh, I thought—" He caught himself and started over. "There you have me, friend. It took us all by surprise. I mean Celia and Alex had their rough moments like any other couple, but when she . . . well, it left us all flabbergasted. She seemed very normal and all. Normal, you know? It fairly tore Alex up. He looked like death himself for a while. I think that party last night was the first time he's really been out of the house since it happened."

"She leave a note?"

"Yeah, she said she just couldn't go on any longer. It was next to her on the car seat. You know how she died?"

"Yes, Reva mentioned it to me."

"Reva." He smiled. "Lovely girl . . . It shocked her, too. She and Celia were very good friends, they were both models. Celia married her artist, and Reva's about to, so I suppose they had a lot of notes to compare on the subject, not that Alex or Leighton are even remotely alike."

"How so?"

"They both paint and wear clothes and eat food, but beyond that they're night and day, stylistically and temperamentally. Like all that business in the studio, it was taken care of with a minimum of fuss and bother in about a quarter hour, right? If you'd gone to Leighton for the work you'd still be talking— and talking. He's more showman than anything. If someone comes to him for a commission he puts them to a lot of trouble so they think they're getting their money's worth. Then he'd have your girl sitting for a couple hours every day for two or three weeks so you think he's really earning his fee."

"That's what we expected with Alex."

"And he didn't give it to you. Art is a business with both of them, but Alex just gets on with it, and if people are disappointed with the lack of show, the finished product makes up for it."

"I'll say. That sketch he did was really great."

"And you don't need to worry about the painting, he'll do something to knock your eyes out."

"How did you two get together?"

He laughed. "It's been so long I hardly remember, we both go so far back. His family had money and mine didn't; he had the polish and I had the spit. I used to get him into a lot of trouble taking him off to pool halls and other fun places, then he'd show me how to look at things and draw them. We both had watercolors down by the time we were out of grade school. He'd won a few prizes and me, too, and then one day I sold something. It convinced me this was a way of making a living without working—that and the occasional crap game."

"And if you left the crap games alone you *could* make a living," said Sandra, coming in with a broom and dustpan. "Is he telling you the sad story of his life, Jack?"

"Not so sad," defended Evan. "I enjoy every moment." To illustrate, he drained off the rest of the beer and raided the box for another. Sandra rolled her eyes in mock suffering and left for the studio.

Evan grinned beatifically. "Before yesterday she'd have given me a five-minute lecture on gambling, drinking, and other forms of peaceable sport. Now she's so occupied with Alex it takes the pressure off me. Isn't love wonderful?"

I had to agree. "She and Alex have known each other just as long?"

"Not really. He was my friend mostly until we got older, then he went off to study in Paris for a couple of years. When he returned she started to notice him, but then he was off to New York getting established. He came back just after the crash; famous, quite thoroughly married to Celia, and off Sandra's eligible list."

"That's a funny way to describe a marriage."

"It applied to them. I liked Celia well enough, but she was a bit self-centered—no, that's not the word. . . ." He eyed the dwindling contents of the beer bottle. "I think this stuff is starting to get to me."

Before he could decide on his definition, Bobbi, Sandra, and Adrian walked in. Bobbi was pulling on her brown velvet gloves.

"All finished?" I asked.

"Jack, you should see the things he has in there, it's absolutely wonderful. Alex should have it in a gallery or museum. They're all too beautiful to be shelved up out of sight."

"Maybe you could talk to Reva," said Evan.

Adrian shrugged it off. "Another time. You're going to see her tomorrow, aren't you?"

"Yeah, sure, first thing, but I'm having my doubts."

"You promised, Evan, so don't try to get out of it," Sandra told him.

"I wouldn't do that, it's just I won't be held responsible if Reva says no. She'll be thinking of Leighton—"

"And Leighton thinks of himself," Adrian concluded, twisting his ring around again.

"Well, it *is* her gallery, of course she'll want to be selling his work and Reva might think my stuff would take away from his sales."

"Even though the gallery gets a commission should your work sell?"

"Not as much as they'd get from Leighton. He's very popular just now, you know."

"We know, but we also know your work is quite different from Leighton's and would attract a different audience. Reva will certainly want to widen the pool of prospective buyers."

"Not that wide . . . Can you imagine someone like Mr. Danube walking in for a look?"

Adrian apparently could and wisely shifted the point of his argument. "Sandra expects you to try."

"I *will* try, I've said so, but . . ."

"Yes?"

"Nothing, just but."

Sandra had her arms crossed and was leaning against a counter, watching the exchange with amusement. "Alex, he's just having a case of the shakes."

"Odd, that usually doesn't happen until the morning after the debauch."

Evan sighed dramatically. "They're talking like I'm not in the room anymore, which means I've become invisible again. If I could learn to control it I'd go on stage and make a fortune."

Sandra came over to put her arm around Evan. "You don't have to worry. Even if Reva says no, it won't diminish your work. You're a wonderful painter; sooner or later more people than just Mr. Danube will realize it."

"Sooner, I hope."

"Right now Leighton is popular with the public, but these things come in cycles. Your turn will come. Look at Impressionism; when it first came out everyone hated it, but now look what it's going for."

"Right, but aren't those artists all dead by now?"

She groaned. "Don't be so morbid, Evan."

5

"SO WHAT DID you think of the higher arts?" I asked as Bobbi finished off the last of her steamed vegetables.

"Not so high. It's a business, just like everything else. But I'm not saying that's bad. Artists have to eat, you know, speaking of which, thanks for supper."

We were in Hallman's, one of Escott's favorite haunts. It was a fancy place with potted palms and a staff that, in their bright uniforms, looked like fugitives from a Russian opera. Though the greatness of its food was forever lost to me, it was still a hell of a good place to impress one's girlfriend.

Bobbi did proper justice to her meal, which somewhat compensated things for our waiter. To keep from insulting him or the chef, I said I'd eaten earlier and pretended to nurse a cup of coffee.

"Sure you don't want a bite?" She offered a forkful dripping in rich sauce.

My throat constricted. "Not of that, no."

"You don't eat anything?"

"'Fraid not."

She caught the look on my face. "Have I said the wrong thing?"

"Not you, sweetheart, you've a right to ask questions. I just don't know if this is a private enough place for me to answer them."

"You really think anyone here would take it seriously?"

"Why take chances?"

"Okay." She shrugged and changed the subject. "What was all that talk you and Evan had in the kitchen?"

"I was just letting him know some of his financial worries were over." I explained about the roughhouse with Dimmy Wallace's boys the night of the party. "Now you know why Sandra and Evan were camping out with Alex."

"How did you get the shark off his back?"

"I talked to Gordy about it and he did all the hard work. Guess I owe him a favor now."

"Maybe. He might not collect."

"Yeah? Why not?"

"Because of all that business with Slick. I think he still feels bad about slugging you around."

"I never felt a thing."

She didn't look convinced.

"Honest, he hardly laid a hand on me."

"Now you're sounding like Evan."

"Let's hope he's not catching. What were all those paintings like that Alex showed you?"

"It's hard to say, you just have to see them. He had everything: mountains, cities, there were dozens of portraits that he'd done for magazines—really famous people."

"And now you're going to be one of them."

"You think having Alex Adrian do my portrait will make me famous?"

"More likely the other way around."

"Why, thanks! But he's already famous."

"And he hasn't worked since January. Sabbaticals like that can ruin a career. You have to keep producing or risk being forgotten."

"Not this guy. His stuff ought to be in a book or something. With someone like him I'll bet hundreds of galleries would jump at the chance to exhibit his work."

"Maybe you can mention it to him during your sittings. Who you taking along for moral support?"

"You were my first choice."

I nodded a modest acknowledgment of my status with her. "And your second?"

"Probably Marza."

"You sure she won't curdle his creative process?"

"She's okay, except where you're concerned."

"Tell me what I've done this time."

"Nothing, as usual. Once Marza has an idea lodged in her head about someone, it's impossible to get it out."

I waved a playful fist. "I know a great way to—"

"It's a lost cause, Jack. She'll either have to get used to you or lump it."

"Lump it," I concluded. "Is it just me or does she hate all men?"

"Well, there's Madison, but I suppose he's so tied up with his politics he doesn't really count. She's not really a man hater, she just hasn't met a nice guy yet."

And with her attitude it seemed likely she never would. Where Marza was concerned, charity was not one of my stronger virtues.

"I think I'll ask Penny instead of Marza," she said thoughtfully. "She's a giggler with nothing in her head but clothes talk, but meeting Alex Adrian might keep her subdued."

"She's the skinny redhead I met at your housewarming?"

"Slender. And yes, that's her. You've got a good memory."

"She nearly dropped her drink on me. I tend to keep track of potential disasters. Just keep her from tipping Alex's paints over, he's got a temper."

"I don't doubt it."

"Why's that?"

"When he was showing me his canvases he came across a portrait of a woman and sort of froze. It was like I was next to a block of ice and I could feel the cold coming off him."

"And you think it was anger?"

She nodded. "Then he shook out of it, shoved the painting back, and brought out something else as though nothing had happened. I wanted to ask him about it, but it wouldn't have been polite, so I pretended not to have noticed. He was aware of it, too; damn social games."

"A portrait, you said?"

"I think it was his wife."

"Why?"

"Just a feeling from the way he acted. It's like those times when you say Charles can read your mind."

Escott was no swami, he just had his own method for figuring out people by the way they talked and moved. It was all based on deliberate and analytical observation and could sometimes be pretty spooky if you're not used to it. Bobbi wasn't as scientific minded, but I could put as much stock in her intuition as Escott's logic. Both were pretty reliable.

The evening ended very pleasantly at Bobbi's and I almost didn't need the elevator to float down to the lobby and out the door. The euphoria was enough that I hardly noticed the ghost-town streets during my leisurely drive to Chicago's huge library. I parked under one of the multi-globed lamps and made a cautious sweep of the area for watchers. The last thing I needed was a beat cop taking notice.

Things were clear and I slipped inside. Literally. Vampirism has disadvantages, but sometimes it can be fun. The whole place was mine, no interruptions, no distractions; all I had to do was remember to get home before dawn, which was hours away yet.

I headed for the newspaper section and located their morgue, searching out all the editions from the previous January. They were very informative about the usual New Year's celebrations and stories on the first babies born after midnight.

The Celia Adrian suicide made the front page on the afternoon of the third. Details were sparse: her husband, the famous painter and magazine illustrator, Alex Adrian, had found her slumped in their car in their closed garage early that morning. The car had apparently been started and left to run until the gas was gone, but by then it was long over. He'd called an ambulance, but efforts to revive her were futile; she'd been dead for some hours.

It gave a few more crumbs about Adrian's career and that was all—no hint of suicide, much less murder.

ADRIAN TURNS VIOLENT! screamed the next day's paper. On the surface the story was of a man so beside himself with strong emotion that it came boiling out onto the streets of his peaceful neighborhood with an attempt to assault a member of the press.

Read between the lines: the reporter had gotten too nosy and Adrian had kicked him out the door.

A day later in one of the tabloids was a picture of Adrian and Celia with the headline question: IS THIS THE PORTRAIT OF A KILLER? The story went on to report again on Celia's death, with heavy emphasis on innuendo. Adrian was not available for comment, the police were keeping quiet, and there was a possibility of further startling developments in the case. The question in the headline was clarified down at the end of the article as they puzzled over the tragedy of Celia Adrian and why she may have killed herself. There was no by-line, which was hardly a surprise.

It was an unfortunate piece, escalating things enough so that the more respectable papers noticed and joined in on the smear. A story on the coroner's report appeared in one, most of it padding. Celia Adrian had died on January 3, between the hours of midnight and four A.M., of asphyxiation caused by carbon monoxide exhaust from her car. The note found beside her on the car was such as to indicate that she had killed herself. No other evidence was available to the contrary, but the tabloid strongly suggested that the police were being lax in their duty. Later I found an editorial with the theme of there being a different kind of justice for the rich and famous as opposed to the poor and oppressed. Stirring stuff, but not so noble when in conjunction with their apparent campaign against Adrian.

There was one last story a day later on Adrian's house being the focus of an innocent prank by some schoolchildren. It vaguely alluded to a broken window that may have been the result of an off-course baseball and condemned Adrian for wasting the resources of the police department in calling their assistance to the scene. This one had a by-line, somebody named Barb Steler, which I noted down before looking for more of her work.

Yesterday's tabloid carried her name, so it wouldn't be too hard to find her, something I had an inclination to do. I wanted to know why she had it in for Adrian.

Flipping back to the screamer headline, I studied the grainy shadows of the photo. It was obviously a file shot, taken at some social function. Adrian was in a tuxedo, the woman next to him wore a shiny evening gown. Celia had a model's aristocratic face; short, light hair; and beautiful, searching eyes. I tried to see if there was a hint of self-destruction in them, but whatever I saw was inevitably my projection onto her. This was a picture in a newspaper, not a crystal ball or even a mirror.

The tabloid offices were larger than I'd expected, but it probably took a large and imaginative staff to keep their pages filled with more than ads for invisible lifts and rejuvenating face creams. It was getting late, but there was still a skeleton crew working the phones and typing up tomorrow's scandals. At the receptionist's desk a large man with a morose, leathery face noticed me come in and stopped eating his horse burger long enough to ask what I wanted.

"I'm looking for Barb Steler."

"Gotta 'pointment?"

"Get serious, at this hour?"

"Then why try here?"

"Thought she might be working late."

"Maybe, but not this shift. Tomorrow she might be in."

"I want to find her now."

"You got that in common with a lot of guys, but I can't help you." He sounded all broken up about it, heaving a sigh and giving me the bracing benefit of the raw onions in his dinner. He made it easier by looking me square in the eye, daring me to start something.

I smiled and leaned in closer. "Listen to me, this is very important . . ."

Like I said, sometimes it can be fun. A minute later I had Barb Steler's home address straight from their personnel files and the advice that she wouldn't be there, but in a boozer down the street called Marty's.

"What's she look like?"

"You'll know her. Only real broad in the joint."

I thanked the man and told him to go back to his meal and forget he ever saw me. He did so, and by the time he shook it enough to be able to notice me again I was out the door.

Marty's was a dark, comfortable place, and its proximity to the tabloid offices must have made it the main watering hole for the workers there. One of the deep, padded leather booths was loaded with a group swapping lies over their drinks. I could tell they were newsmen a mile off because I used to do the same thing. A big brown case on the floor identified at least one of them as a photographer. They'd sooner be hanged than part with their Speed Graphics, on or off duty.

I was about to ask the bartender for help when I saw Barb Steler. Her co-worker had been right when he said I'd know her, and it wasn't just because she was the only woman in the place. No mental image I had conjured would have fit the reality.

She was in the booth with the boys, blowing cigarette smoke with the best and holding her own in the conversation. She wore a severely tailored suit, a mannish hat, and a worldly expression. Her bronze eyes were very large and predatory rather than vulnerable. Her skin' was the palest I'd ever seen, but didn't look unhealthy. It set off her short jet black hair and generous bright red mouth.

I must have been gaping; she saw me and those seeking eyes flicked up and down and then turned to one of her party.

"Friend of yours, Taylor?" she drawled in a husky voice that could carry. She had meant it to do so.

Taylor gave me a once-over and shook his head. "You got a problem, buddy?"

"Barb Steler?" I said, making it less of a question than a statement. I ignored Taylor because I hate drunks.

"Give the kid a nickel," said Taylor, and got a chorus of approval from the audience.

"Who wants to know?" she asked.

"My name's Jack Fleming and I'd like to talk to you for a moment."

"You and half of Chicago," added Taylor. More hilarity.

"About what?" There was a hint of a smile, but it was a distant hint.

"I'd rather not say." Weak, but it was the best bait I could come up with under the circumstances. The way I'd said it indicated I had something interesting to tell and that she might not want to share it with her gin-soaked colleagues.

She tilted her head to one side, studying me with amusement. I studied her right back and she didn't seem to mind.

Taylor got impatient at all the eye play. "Ya want us to throw the bum out, Barb?"

This didn't speed up her decision; she'd already made it by then, but it did give her an excuse to act. She gestured with one hand, the way queens do when they wave at their subjects, and damned if every one of the guys there didn't give way to it. Two of them made haste to clear the booth so she could slide out.

I expected her to be tall; it had to do with her long, graceful neck and the way she moved. Again, I thought of royalty.

The boys were watching us with some resentment. She knew it but left the next move to me. I tried a cool but polite smile and nodded at some empty booths at the far end of the joint. She matched the smile and preceded me slowly, giving me plenty of time to evaluate the body under the suit. There wasn't a thing wrong with it.

She eased into a booth and I took the other side, facing her.

"Drink?" she asked.

"What would you like?"

"It was an offer, not a request."

"Thanks, but I'll take a rain check. You need anything?"

"Not to drink, no. What is it you wanted to talk to me about, Mr. Fleming?"

"Last January did you cover the story on Celia Adrian's suicide?"

"Among others. Why do you ask?"

"I was interested in why your paper maintained that it might not have been suicide."

The amusement spread from her huge eyes down to her mouth. She had absolutely perfect teeth. "Because a simple suicide does not sell papers."

"And courting a libel suit does?"

"Of course." Her cigarette burned out and she made a point of thoroughly crushing the butt in the table ashtray. "Now, why are you so interested in such old news? Surely you're not a lawyer?"

"No, I'm a journalist. I'm working on a book about famous unsolved cases and I thought the Adrian thing might be something to look into."

"It sounds very ambitious."

"It fills in the time."

"What paper do you work for?"

I gave her the name. "Except I don't work for them anymore. I came into a legacy, decided to quit and go free-lance." It was the truth, more or less. I was a crummy liar.

"Aren't you the lucky one? That's a New York paper. . . . Why are you out here?"

"Because this is where the story happened. What can you tell me about it that didn't get past the editor?"

She made a business of lighting another cigarette and blowing the smoke from her nose. It was quite leisurely and gave her plenty of time to think. "Very little, really. It was a fairly simple case, as I remember, but this was months ago. You probably know more about what I wrote than I do if you've been into the old files."

"I guess so, but that's not quite the same as listening to someone who's been there. What were your impressions of Alex Adrian?"

"The husband? He hardly left any."

Somehow it was oddly comforting to know I wasn't the only bad liar in the world. Her answer complicated things, but I had all night. "Too bad, I was really interested in hearing something solid. I guess I can check the police records tomorrow."

"Yes, there's always tomorrow, isn't there?" She was smiling again and part of me felt like a lone fish in a shark tank.

"I suppose I should leave you and let you get back to your friends."

"They can wait, Mr. Fleming."

"My name is Jack."

"I know, and mine is Barb." She locked those wonderful eyes onto mine again.

This opened things up for a little flirting, but not much—she was a very decisive woman. She stood up soon after and went back to the boys long enough to toss a dollar on the table to cover her drink, and we left together.

"Think she'll let this one live out the night?" Taylor muttered to the others as the door closed behind us.

The pretext we'd established between ourselves was for me to give her a ride home. We walked to my car and I helped her in; it was all very formal and polite. I never liked playing games like that, but this time I didn't mind because I wanted her information.

She had a nice apartment in a nice building. Thankfully she didn't pause at the door for more games on whether she should let in me or not. She opened it and let me make up my own mind and smiled again as I let it snick shut behind me.

"I suppose you think I'm fast?" she said, tugging at the fingers of her black kid gloves. She tossed the empties onto a chair along with her purse and hat.

"I think you know what you want," I returned.

She vanished into the kitchen and I heard the clink of ice on glass. When she came out the top few buttons of her coat were undone, revealing a little more milk white skin. Her very short hair and the harsh lines of her suit perversely emphasized her femininity. It was the same kind of effect Marlene Dietrich got in a tuxedo.

She handed me a glass heavy with ice and bourbon. "Bottoms up?"

It was less a toast than an invitation. She sipped, watching me over the rim, then eased onto her couch and watched me some more. I let my lips touch the edge of the glass and was hard put to hide the spasm of rejection my stomach sent up.

"You don't have to have it if you don't like it." Innuendo was her specialty.

"Thanks." I placed it on a low table and sat next to her. We weren't quite touching.

She put down her drink and rested her arm along the back of the couch, her fingers lightly rubbing the fabric of my coat. "You know, most men your age would either be all over me at this point or rushing out the door in a desperate attempt to preserve their virtue."

"Which do you prefer?"

"Neither, that's why you're here. You act older than you look."

"Maybe I am."

"Are you really a journalist?"

"Not anymore."

"Perhaps you thought by coming here I might talk a little more freely about Alex Adrian?"

I laughed a little. "Not much gets past you."

"No, indeed. I'm afraid you'll find me quite useless, as I've nothing to tell you. Nothing at all."

We had moved closer together somehow. "That's too bad."

Her mouth curled. "What would your girlfriend think if she saw you like this?"

"Who says I've got a girlfriend?"

"I do. I can smell her perfume on you. Winter Rose. It's very expensive."

She pressed the length of her body against mine, and I won't lie and say she wasn't having her effect on me. My symptoms were familiar enough: tunnel vision, heightened hearing and smell, and of course my upper canines were pushing themselves out of their retractable pockets. Mixed in with Bobbi's perfume and Barb's perfume was the all-too-tantalizing scent of blood. I stopped breathing but couldn't shut out its soft rumble as it surged through the veins in her throat.

She sensed at least part of what was happening to me and brought her lips around to cover mine. It lasted only an instant and left the possibility open for more if I wished it. I did, but pulled back.

"You don't have to do this."

She smiled with infinite patience. "How many times do I have to convince a man that it's not a question of 'have to'? I want to and that should be enough. Now lie back and enjoy yourself." And she pushed herself against me a little and started undoing my tie.

I let things go until she stopped to smile at me again. She slipped into it easily; it was so subtle I was only aware she was under by the slightly glazed look in her bronze eyes. Her hands dropped away and her head went sleepily back, drawing the skin tight over her unblemished throat. I stroked it gently, feeling the vein working under my fingers and noting the soft warmth with a great deal of regret.

Getting to my feet, I walked around the living room until things settled down internally. A few gulps of fresh air from an open window helped clear my head and before long my teeth were back in their place again. Barb Steler was one of the most desirable women I'd ever met, and I certainly wanted her, but she wasn't Bobbi and there was no way in the world that I would ever intentionally hurt either of them.

With that firmly in mind I went back to the couch and sat next to her. Her eyes were wide open, but she was asleep, and taking no notice of me now.

"Barb, close your eyes and think back to last January. I want you to tell me about the story you did on Alex Adrian."

Her eyes drifted shut. It was more for my comfort than hers, because I hate that empty look they get.

"Tell me about Alex Adrian."

Her face twisted. "Bastard."

For a second I wondered if she was talking about him or me, but she was still safely under. "Why is he a bastard?"

"He doesn't love me."

I didn't quite whistle. "You love him?"

She made a low noise in her throat. That was one question she didn't want to answer.

"Okay, never mind. Where did you first meet him?"

"Paris."

"When he was a student there?"

"Yes."

"Tell me about it."

It took quite a while because I had to prompt her with questions. It was a simple story but she'd buried it down deep.

She was a society deb on a continental tour with some friends when one of them dared her to model for an art class. She took up the dare and so met Alex Adrian, a promising art student. Long after her friends returned to the States she was still living with him in a little hotel on the Left Bank. Things were idyllic, from her point of view at least. There had been talk of marriage for a time, but it had fallen through.

"He didn't really want me," she sighed. "He didn't. It was his art first, always his goddamned art."

Their fights became more frequent as she demanded more attention from him, and he pulled away to concentrate on his studies. She finally left for home, returning to her own study of journalism. She was smart enough and good enough to work for any paper in the country, but preferred the style of her tabloid. She had a lot of venom in her system and it only increased when Adrian returned from New York with his new wife.

I shook my head, not liking my next question. "Do you think he killed her?"

"No . . ."

"Barb, tell me, did you kill her?"

"No."

"So it was suicide, after all?"

"Yes."

"And all those stories in the paper?"

"He deserved it. He hurt me. Bastard."

From under her closed lids a tear slipped out and trickled down her heart-shaped face. I touched it away.

"You tired, Barb?"

"Yes."

"I don't blame you. I want you to get up and get ready for bed as usual. All right?"

Her eyes opened and, still unaware of me, she walked into her bedroom and began removing her clothes. It took some effort on my part to remember I was a gentleman. I stayed out in the living room until she'd finished her bath and climbed into bed. The springs creaked as she settled into the sheets and pulled up the blanket.

She wore an ice white satin gown that left her shoulders bare and defined her breasts. She didn't see me standing in the doorway, but stared at something next to it. I came into the room. Hanging on the wall was an oil portrait of her. She was younger, her hair was different, but the artist had left no doubt to the world about her beauty. The signature at the bottom was Alex Adrian's.

"Bastard," she whispered.

I walked around the big double bed and pulled back the covers from the empty spot next to her and climbed in, clothes and all. It was the only way I could think of to convincingly leave the impression we'd slept together.

"Barb—"

"Barbara. My full name is Barbara."

I put an arm around her and drew her close so she was leaning against me. "Barbara."

"Yes?"

"You hide it very well, but you hurt a lot because of him."

"Yes."

"I think you should let go of the hurt, don't you?"

Until she crumpled, I hadn't been aware of the tension in her muscles. I murmured things to her, soft words meant to soothe, and they seemed to work. When her eyes were dry again, she really was ready to sleep. I shifted position, sitting up and facing her and easing her back onto the pillow.

"You had a good evening, Barbara," I told her. "You don't have to remember talking to me about Adrian, but thinking about him doesn't hurt now. Understand?"

She nodded.

"Now you have a good night's sleep. When you wake up in the morning you'll feel a lot better about things."

The covers rustled as she turned over. I carefully got out of bed and studied the portrait a moment longer before shutting off the light. A minute later I locked her apartment door, slipped out into the hall, and walked quietly downstairs so as not to disturb the other tenants.

The car seemed to make more noise starting than usual, but only because I wanted it not to. I shifted gears gently and drifted down the dark and empty morning streets, my head full of complicated thoughts and feelings. Instead of the road I saw a heart-shaped young face in an expensive frame.

The sad part was that she'd been dead wrong about Adrian; no one could paint a portrait like that and not be in love.

6

THE KITCHEN PHONE started jangling just as consciousness returned and my eyes popped open. Escott caught it on the third ring and I could tell by his end of the conversation that it was Bobbi. I threw on a bathrobe and decided to spare his nerves and walk up the basement steps in the regular way. He handed over the earpiece and went back to the front room to finish listening to his radio program.

Bobbi was anything but calm. "That rat backed out!" she stated, her voice vibrating with fury. "He called me up this afternoon to call off the sittings."

She'd said enough for me to identify the rat in question. "What happened? Did he say why?"

"He just said he tried and couldn't get into it, after all, some stuff about not being ready to get back to painting yet."

"That's ridiculous, after the way he was last night?"

"I know. First he can't wait to start, now he dumps the whole thing. What's the matter with the man?"

The thought flashed through my head that Barb Steler had remembered our talk last night and somehow made trouble with Adrian. It was worry making, but extremely unlikely. I'd been very careful with her. "Give me time to dress and I'll pick you up. We'll go over for a little talk and try to straighten things out."

"Are you sure you want me along? I feel like strangling him."

"Fine, I'll probably help."

Escott's voice drifted in after I hung up. "Problem?" he asked casually.

I shoved my hands in the robe's pockets and hunched into the front room. He was at his ease on the long sofa and stretched out a lazy arm to turn the radio down. I spent a minute or so explaining about the portrait commission and Adrian's sudden refusal of it.

He cocked a philosophical eyebrow. "Artistic temperament, perhaps? Perhaps not. He's probably far too professional to indulge in such games."

"I don't know. I'm taking Bobbi over to find out."

"A suggestion?"

"Yeah?"

"Take along your receipt—just in case you can't change his mind." His hand swung back to the volume dial again.

With him it was a suggestion with double meaning, a nudge for my conscience to kick in, as if it needed much help. I *had* been thinking of influencing Adrian, but recognized with some sourness that Escott had a point, at least for the moment.

Bobbi was dressed for war in a severe black suit with a slash of bloodred color on her compressed lips. She was already waiting in the lobby, and as soon as my car stopped she shot out and yanked the door open.

"I'm mad," she said, quite unnecessarily. Anyone in a fifty-yard radius could figure it out easily enough.

"We'll see what's going on."

"He chickened out, that's what I think." She crossed her arms and glared out the front window. "And it's just not fair."

I got the car rolling again and listened as she talked herself down from a long afternoon of anger and frustration. By the time we reached Adrian's she'd calmed somewhat and was willing to hear his side of things, if he had one.

He took his time answering the door and there was a change in him. The relaxed face we'd seen last night had been replaced by the guarded go-to-hell-and-so-what expression I'd noted at the party. It took Bobbi by surprise; she was all wound up to ask an obvious question or two, but one look and she knew it was a lost cause.

He let us into the entryway, but no farther. On a table rested the envelope with the money, which he handed to me, meeting my eyes, expecting a reproach and not caring.

"I can't really explain it," he said. "I just know I can't do the job, after all."

"Why not?"

He'd been ready for that question, and the answer came out easily enough. "Do you ever get a writer's block, if that's what you call it? I've the same thing, but for painting."

It wasn't something I could argue with; you can't force a person to create against their will. You also can't ask them why when they don't want to talk. I couldn't, not with Bobbi looking on. I gave him his receipt without another word. He stared at it, something crossing his face as if it were the end of the world, then shoved the piece of paper into his pocket.

"I'm sorry to have put you both to so much trouble," he said tonelessly. He was saying what was expected of him; whether he meant it or not was anyone's guess.

Bobbi shot me a brief look of alarm, her instincts were doing overtime. I nodded back, we'd talk later.

Adrian opened the door for us and we were back on the porch with it closing quietly behind. I heard his steps retreating deep into the house.

"We sure read him the riot act, didn't we?" she said. "He looked positively sick."

"He was like that when I first met him, but he perked up when Sandra was around."

"You think they had a fight?"

"You think it's really our business?"

"No, but I'd like to find out."

We got into the car and I drove half a block and parked by a small neighborhood grocery at the corner. "Would you mind waiting here for a little while? I want to go back and check on him?"

"Because he might do something?" Apparently, she had the same idea about suicide as I did.

"I just want to check." And make sure there were no

dangling ropes or sleeping pills within reach. Bobbi said she'd be all right and I got out and walked back down the street, trying not to look conspicuous. It still felt as though every window had a face in it and that every barking dog was reacting to me alone. Passing under an especially large tree, its trunk thick with shadow, I disappeared.

Adrian's house was exactly on my left. I willed myself in that direction and pushed against the light wind until stopped by a wall of wood. I pressed harder and was through the wall, floating in the still air of his front room and drifting around to find a safe place to solidify. Invisibility is not as much fun as you'd think: with my sight gone and my hearing a joke, all I had was extended touch, which could be deceptive. After a minute of covering the four corners and not getting any sense of another presence, I decided to risk it and materialize.

The risk paid off, for the room was empty and dark. I listened hard and could just pick up the sound of his breathing elsewhere. Cautious and as silent as possible, I edged into the hall. The rooms that were in view were also dark, except for the kitchen, which had a small light burning wanly over the stove. Beyond the kitchen was his studio.

I vanished again and floated in. He seemed to be lying on the couch. By moving close I could tell which way he was facing and was able to get behind him and out of his line of sight. I solidified in a crouch, though, just in case I threw a shadow from the banks of windows behind me.

The only light came from a small work lamp caged from one of his tables. Its gooseneck was twisted so the illumination fell on a canvas clamped onto his easel. It was a portrait of Celia Adrian. The newspaper photo had been a decent likeness at least of how she looked—Adrian had recorded who she had been. The style was the same as Barb Steler's portrait, but more mature and assured.

I saw guarded happiness in the blue eyes, a hint of selfishness around the mouth, and an unearthly beauty in every stroke of his brush. It was truth and idealization all at once. Her faults were there, but accepted as part of the whole. He'd loved her dearly, but not blindly.

The figure on the couch moved only a little. He was smoking

slowly, thoughtfully, and I could spend all night speculating on those thoughts. For now he didn't seem on the verge of doing away with himself or anyone else. My curiosity was satisfied to some extent, but with Bobbi waiting, there was no time for a more thorough investigation. Maybe later I could pay him a less hurried visit.

She'd left the car for the grocery. Through the sign-covered windows I could see her nodding and listening to the middle-aged woman behind the counter. After a few minutes Bobbi picked up her package and joined me.

"You're not the only one who's a detective," she said, sliding into the car.

"I'm only an assistant to a private agent. You call Charles a detective and he'll come out in hives."

"Whatever. I got the lady inside talking about Alex and his wife's death."

"So was it suicide or murder?"

"About half and half. She used to wait on his wife, 'a tall, pretty lady who'd give you the time of day when you asked,' and can't imagine she would have done such a wicked thing. On the other hand, living with an artist can't be all that easy."

"Did you ask her about the day when it happened?"

"She said she saw the ambulance and wondered what the fuss was about and was terribly shocked to learn Mrs. Adrian was dead. She'd read all the papers and when they started saying Alex murdered her she was ready to believe it. He came into her store about a week later and she was ready to throw him out until she saw his face."

"Like death warmed over?"

"You heard?"

"He had the same effect on us tonight, remember?"

"Vividly. I was ready to kill him and then it just seemed so useless, there was nothing there to argue with."

We both nodded in silent agreement. "What now?"

She looked surprised. "We go see Sandra and Evan. I didn't buy this just for my voice, you know." She shifted the bag and I caught the subtle clink of beer bottles inside.

Our knock on Evan's door got no answer, but I was sure I heard a voice and a soft thump.

"Think they're out?" Bobbi asked.

"Someone's there." I put an ear to the door but couldn't really distinguish much through it. We knocked louder and got no answer. "Maybe Francis came back to try and beat him up again, after all."

She tried the knob, but the door was locked. "The super might have a key—"

"You ever see my vanishing act?"

"Your what?"

"It makes Charles nervous and I didn't want to give you heart failure."

"You mean you can just . . . ?" She made vague gestures. I'd done it once before in her presence, but it had been dark and rainy and she may have missed it, having other things on her mind at the time.

"Yeah, wanna see?"

She was a game girl. "Okay . . ."

Then I wasn't there anymore. As though wrapped in cotton, I heard her gasp of surprise. I slipped inside, went solid, and unlocked the door. She jumped when it swung open, but her short blond hair wasn't quite on end.

"Yeeps! How'd you do that? I thought you were supposed to turn into a fog or something."

I pointed an accusing finger. "You've been reading Stoker again, haven't you?"

"Never mind that, why'd you never tell me about this?"

"You never asked."

"But—"

"Shh, I want to listen."

Now that we were inside, neither of us had much trouble hearing things. Somewhere in the back Evan laughed and a girl's voice responded, "That's right, now I'll hold it here and you shove it in."

Bobbi's mouth popped open and she blushed a bright red.

"No, not that way!" the girl complained. "Smoother . . . get that flap as well."

Flap? Bobbi mouthed the word.

"It can wait a minute," said Evan. "I thought I heard something out front."

"You just don't want to do a little honest work," was the retort.

Evan strolled in wearing a baggy set of mustard yellow golf pants, red shoes, and orange-and-green argyle socks topped off by an ancient paint-smeared shirt. His surprise from seeing us quickly translated into a smile. "Jack! Bobbi! Welcome to my extremely humble home, come in."

"If we're interrupting anything—"

"Nah, it's too late for that or I'd have kicked you out. I thought I'd locked the door anyway, oh well. My friend Sally was just helping me with the linens. It seems I don't know how to make a proper hospital corner."

Sally also strolled in, a petite girl with rich brown hair and a lush figure under her light print dress. She was the maid Evan had been chatting with in the kitchen while his clothes dried. It looked as though the party hadn't been a total disaster for him, after all. Evan introduced us and Bobbi brought out the beer.

"This is great, what's the occasion?" he asked.

"Call it a homecoming gift," said Bobbi. "Where's Sandra?"

"Out somewhere, probably with Alex."

"We were just there, she wasn't with him."

Evan shrugged. "Shopping, then, or at one of her girlfriends' talking about shopping. She'll be back before long. It's all right, she doesn't like beer." He found an opener and popped some caps. Just in time I stopped him from wasting one on me.

"How was Alex when you left today?" I asked.

"Rancid as ever. Why?"

"Because he called Bobbi this afternoon and canceled the portrait commission. When we went by he looked—"

"Like death warmed over," completed Bobbi.

"Really? You mean he decided not to do the painting, just like that?"

I nodded. "We thought you might have an idea why."

"Me?"

"Or Sandra. Did they have any disagreements, stuff like that?"

"No, pretty much the opposite, from what I could tell. They

keep going the way they are and I'll have this rat palace all to myself in another month." Rat palace or not, he seemed very pleased with the prospect.

"Evan, I had an idea that Alex may have taken on the commission in order to help you out with Dimmy Wallace."

He shook his head. "He wouldn't have to do that, he's got plenty of savings. If I asked him for help he'd just give me the money but I haven't asked him for help. Cheating the bookies is one thing, but Alex is my friend, more or less."

"He said he had a painter's block—"

"Not him . . . well, maybe him. There's a first time for everyone, I suppose."

"Sandra said he hadn't painted since his wife died."

"There's a difference between a block and just choosing not to work. He's been sitting around feeling sorry for himself and wondering if he could have made things different for Celia. You ask me, you should go back and give him a kick in the pants and tell him to paint."

"You really think he'd respond to that?"

"Of course he'd respond . . . but I'd want to be there to see the fight." He looked like Sandra for a second with the impishness in his eyes. "This isn't like him, you know. I've never known him to back out of a commission once the money's down. I really can't say what's wrong with him. . . ."

"We could go back and ask this time," suggested Bobbi. "Could you come with us?"

He thought about it, but shook his head. "I'm not too comfortable about that; he's a friend, but this isn't really my business, after all. I'll be honest about things: if Alex turns down the commission, I might have a chance to take his place. . . ."

If anyone else had said it they might have sounded grabby, but not Evan.

"Of course it won't be an Alex Adrian, and I can't charge his price, but it'd be the best I could do."

I shrugged reasonably. "We'll see what works out."

It was enough for him. "Great, now I've got to put on a cleaner shirt and walk Sally home."

"We can drive you—" I offered.

He held up a hand. "Thanks, but we really would like to walk. Why don't you take Bobbi to dinner in the meantime. She's looking a little peaked and you don't want to lose those skin tones."

Sally shifted and looked jealous until he put an arm around her and squeezed.

"Keep 'em enthralled, darling," he told her. "Show off some of my paintings." He ducked into the back of the flat for his shirt.

"I don't know if I can tell you much about them," Sally confessed.

"Paintings usually speak for themselves. If you have to explain them then the artist needs a new job." I was practically quoting what I'd learned from Sandra.

She smiled and laughed and led us to a corner of the room, where dozens of odd-sized canvases were stored vertically in a home-built shelving unit. We pulled out one after another and I got a pretty good idea why Evan wouldn't be making much money on his work. It was beautiful stuff, the colors were rich and all over, but for the most part you couldn't make out what they were representing.

He had a few of what I would call regular paintings. He could indeed please the public if he wished, but he was more comfortable creating his own inner world than recording the one around him. Bobbi discovered an especially large work and tilted it against the wall so she could stand back and get a good look. Sally joined her and both their faces were pinched with puzzlement. All I saw were swirls of fleshy pinks, darker reds, and other warm colors. It looked like another abstract to me. Evan came out, tucking in his shirt.

"That's my favorite, too, ladies."

"What's the title?" asked Bobbi, who was also trying not to ask what it was.

"No title, really, but it is a portrait of a dear old friend of mine. It represents his joy to be meeting another friend he likes very much."

"I don't really see it," said Sally.

"There's a trick to it, actually. You have to stand at a specific spot for the meaning to become clear." He put an arm around each of their shoulders and pulled them back about ten feet from the canvas and stepped away. They stared at it, then suddenly broke into twin shrieks of laughter and outrage. Evan beamed.

I was about five feet from the painting and stepped behind the convulsing girls to get a look—and saw nothing but colors.

"Now you're too far away," he told me, and urged me forward another foot.

It said a lot for his technical skill as a painter that he was able to create such an effect. Too close, it was nothing but colors, too distant and it was more of the same. Stand exactly ten feet away and you could see it for the large-scale and quite rude self-portrait it was.

"He's got very good manners and never fails to rise in the presence of a lovely lady. It's one of my best works," he admitted without a trace of modesty. In the case of this painting, modesty would have been totally out of place.

Bobbi turned down a second night at Hallman's, stating she was too hungry to wait for things to simmer. We found a less pretentious eatery and she made short work of a basic plate of meat and vegetables. This time I didn't bother pretending with a cup of coffee and watched her with enjoyment. She was still snickering about Evan's masterpiece.

"I don't know where he got the nerve to paint it."

"Perhaps he was inspired."

"It certainly explains the number of nudes he had."

"Offended?"

"Nah, that kind of stuff doesn't bother me, it just takes a little getting used to. I may take one of my girlfriends over, she might want to buy it."

"Who is she?"

"None of your business. She's a man-eater and you're the last person I want her to meet."

"What, you don't trust me?" I sounded wounded.

"I trust you, I also have to protect you. She runs through men like I run through silk stockings and leaves them lying around torn up and ready to be thrown away."

"You're more tidy than that."

"Stinker. What's the time?"

"Nine-ten."

"We better not leave it too late."

"I'm ready when you are."

"I know," she said with some smugness, which did wonders for my ego.

For the second time that night we pulled up to Adrian's house. His car was gone.

"A person could get tired of disappointments like this," Bobbi growled.

"Feel like waiting a while?"

"Like for a stakeout?"

"I dunno, I've never been on one of those before."

"Wonder why he left."

So did I, and her question hung uncomfortably in the air between us for the next few minutes.

A car turned down the street, its headlights flashing across the rearview mirror. It slowed and swung into Adrian's driveway. He got out, a carton of cigarettes in his hand, glared at us, and slammed the door of his coupe. He seemed to debate whether he should ignore us and go on in the house or face us and get it over with. We got out of our car and saved him the trouble of deciding.

He waited until we were close enough for him not to have to raise his voice. Along the street curtains had twitched with the slam of the door.

"Yes?" Very polite and ice cold with irritation.

"We came from Evan's," I said.

He blinked, the opening didn't make sense and he had to shift mental gears trying to figure out what I was talking about.

"He said we should come back and kick you in the pants and tell you to start painting again."

He shook his head with exasperation. "Yes, I'm sure he did. Evan needs to learn to mind his own business." He moved past us and unlocked his front door, but indicated we would not be welcome past the threshold. "I've explained myself and tried to apologize. As far as I'm concerned the subject is closed."

Inside his house the phone started ringing, an excuse to leave us, which he gratefully seized. I was feeling pigheaded, though, and followed him inside, with Bobbi right behind. If it came down to it, I was prepared to put him under, even with her looking on. Hell, if we were intimate enough for sex she could survive watching me hypnotize someone.

He glared at us from the phone stand in the front hall, his attention divided by our presence and the need to hear the voice on the other end of the wire.

"What? Yes, what's wrong?" He focused on the phone, his glare shifting back to irritation. "No, I can't now. . . . Then, tell me what it is—oh, all right. I'm on my way." He dropped the receiver onto the cradle in disgust. "That was Evan," he said. "There's some kind of trouble, but he won't say what. I have to leave now."

"Dimmy Wallace?"

He shrugged. "I don't know, but he was very upset." Without another word he pushed past us and held the door long enough for us to get out, then locked it and went to his car.

"Are we going, too?" asked Bobbi.

"Yeah, but if things get too hot, you stay in the car and keep down."

We piled into my Buick and followed him to Evan's house. I was annoyed at the interruption as well. Though I hadn't been able to pick up Evan's side of the conversation, some of the stress-filled tones of his voice had leaked out; enough to make me uneasy.

Evan was sitting on the steps outside, his hands hanging slack and his head down. Adrian was out of his car and striding up to him before I'd set my brakes. By the time I was out Adrian was already going up to the flat.

Bobbi got out with me. I checked both ends of the street, but didn't see anything remotely resembling a bookie's collector. We hurried up to Evan, who took no notice of our arrival. A strong fist closed around my gut and more than anything I wanted to take Bobbi and get out of there.

Evan began to shake his head. A thin keening sound rose from his huddled form and put my back hairs up. Bobbi looked from him to me, her face dead white with alarm.

"What . . . ?"

I spread my hands a little and gestured at the house. Answers would be in there, not with Evan. We went inside and then I told Bobbi in no uncertain terms to stay on the bottom landing while I went up. She didn't argue and kept an eye on Evan.

The stairs creaked with each quick step. In other parts of the house the tenants made their noises of living: a baby gurgled somewhere in the back, on my left a radio blared an ad for a cold remedy. Drifting down from the floors above was the hiss and smell of frying cabbage and bacon. I could not sort out Adrian's individual sounds from the others yet.

The door to the Robley flat was wide open and the lights were on. Now I was able to focus down and heard Adrian's quiet breathing and nothing else. The background of the flat's front room was unchanged: Evan's portrait still leaned against a far wall and a few empty beer bottles cluttered a low table.

New details impressed themselves into the overall picture: some packages carelessly dropped on a chair, a glove on the table, another on the floor, her purse on its side, a tortoiseshell comb fallen from it.

Sandra was on her back in the center of the room, her head turned to one side, her eyes and mouth slightly open.

Adrian was on one knee next to her. He slowly looked up as I entered. He saw me and forgot me because the shock had firmly closed over him. His face was utterly blank and the physical wall I'd seen and felt once before was back, perhaps this time to stay. Walls had their uses, and shutting out unbearable pain was one of them.

He turned to her and with a steady hand gently stroked back a lock of her russet hair. Blood came away on his fingers, but he didn't seem to notice.

7

HE DIDN'T RESPOND to his name, not at first, and I didn't want to have to go in and pull him out.

"She's dead," he stated faintly.

"I know, Alex. Please come away." God, it was surprising how calm I sounded. "Alex. Now."

His hand stopped, hovering just above her still face. I thought he was going to shut her eyes. The fingers drew back. Delicately. He abruptly stood up and swung toward me, or rather the door. I moved aside to let him pass and listened as he went downstairs. Bobbi asked him a question and got no answer. It was a very strong wall. I couldn't blame him for it.

I backed out and followed, utterly heartsick and with knees like jelly.

"Jack?"

Bottom of the stairs. Bobbi's arms. Her warmth, her living warmth. I said something to her, answering her question, and held on to her a little longer. When the worst was over, I was just able to talk.

"This is going to be a mess. Do you want to go home?"

"I can't."

"You can. You haven't really seen anything. The police—"

She shook her head firmly. "I need to be here."

And I was the one who needed her. I pulled her close again, then reluctantly broke away to knock on the super's door down the hall. He was a little peach-colored man with flyaway gray hair clinging to the back of his scalp. I told him that I had an emergency and needed to use his phone. He looked at me and at Bobbi standing forlornly next to the stairs. He seemed about to ask something, then shrugged and let me in. He got all the answers he needed as he listened to my end of the conversation.

The first to come were two uniformed cops; a few minutes later Escott arrived. I'd called him first, but he had the longer drive. Before the uniforms knew he was there he slipped inside the building and was upstairs for a quick look. He came down more slowly, his face somber.

"What do you know?" he asked.

In low tones we told him what we could of the evening, which didn't amount to much, as far as I could see. Just as I finished, one of the cops came up and asked for our story. His partner was trying to question Evan, who was still huddled out on the steps shaking his head. Adrian watched them both, his face expressionless. I repeated it all again, but more simply, and Bobbi corroborated. By the time he'd finished taking notes a car with two detectives pulled up.

The cop went out to talk to them, then held the door as a well-built man in expensively cut clothes stepped out.

Escott glanced at me, one brow raised.

"Thought it'd be a good idea to call someone we know," I said.

"It cannot hurt," he agreed.

I'd specifically talked to Lieutenant Blair despite the fact that the last time I'd seen him he'd been one short step away from booking me for murder. We'd worked things out, sort of, but he had no memory of how I'd convinced him to let me go. He only knew we were friends. At the time I'd felt like a heel for artificially inducing the friendship, but now it seemed more like a good investment.

Blair walked around Evan, looked Adrian up and down, then came over to us. We didn't shake hands, it wouldn't have been appropriate. He nodded at Escott.

"Charles. Thought you might turn up since Jack phoned it in."

Escott nodded back. "I'm here solely as moral support."

"Sure you are." He went to one side with the cop who questioned me and listened to him, then made the pilgrimage upstairs. More uniforms appeared and followed, keeping emerging tenants out of the way and asking more questions.

Hours later they were still asking them, but not making much progress. They'd taken over the super's flat. He didn't seem to mind, it was the most excitement he'd seen since Lindbergh landed.

Evan sat in the borrowed kitchen, his eyes hollow and staring at nothing. He was as cold sober as the stale cup of coffee in front of him, and still in shock. Adrian was the same, but able to respond to things in a slow way. Some time earlier he'd formally identified the body, his voice flat and soulless as he pronounced her name. Now he stood bolt upright with his arms crossed and his back pressed to a squat icebox, watching Evan, but not really seeing him.

Escott, Bobbi, and I had found a corner and quietly talked. I filled him in on the fight with Francis Koller and Toumey and all the business of the portrait and some of the business with Barb Steler. The latter had been judiciously edited since Bobbi was listening, but I would have done that anyway.

"And you say he must have gone out for cigarettes?" Escott murmured, carefully not looking at Adrian.

"That's what he had in his hand when he drove up. I know what you're thinking, Charles."

"It's just a thought, and certainly not the only possibility open to us, but all have to be considered."

"Let's try considering something else," said Bobbi. "He may have had the time to do it—it was at least an hour between us leaving with Evan and getting to Alex's—but you're short on motive."

"For Adrian, but motives may also be found in the best of families." Escott's eyes flicked in Evan's direction. Bobbi gave him a look that would have burned through steel. He took it stoically enough but did not retract the suggestion. "The police are well aware of that fact and are of the opinion that she *did* know her killer. From the little Lieutenant Blair has shared with me—"

Her eyes flared again. "But he *couldn't*—look at the poor man—"

"I know, but it might be interpreted as guilt, mightn't it?" Before she could reply he mitigated it all with a brief, dismissive gesture. "I'm only looking at this from their point of view. As yet, neither they nor we have enough data to work with, a circumstance I am more than willing to remedy. When the police are finished questioning the other tenants, I'll have a turn. Jack, you might find a conversation with Lieutenant Blair to be profitable."

"He'll be wanting to talk with us anyway. I'll see what I can get."

"Good man."

He started to say something else, but there was a muted commotion in the hallway and all eyes except Evan's turned toward the open door. Two beefy men were thumping heavily down the stairs. No one spoke as they carried the long wicker basket past the door and out into the night. I felt Bobbi's slim hand grip my arm tightly and she gulped breath back as the reality of Sandra's death hit her all over again. She had taken it all quietly enough when I'd broken the news to her, but there's a big difference between hearing and seeing.

She continued to hold on to my arm and stare long after they'd gone. Her reaction troubled Escott as well, and he covered the back of her other hand lightly with his long fingers, waking her from it.

"I'm very sorry," he told her.

Bobbi had been dry eyed until now. Escott's compassion tipped things for her and her lips trembled and twisted. I offered my handkerchief and she dabbed at the tears that suddenly spilled out. It was all very quiet and over in a minute; she'd wait for more privacy before really letting go with her grief.

Lieutenant Blair had followed the body down and now stood in the doorway, his dark eyes traveling and pausing on each of us. He murmured something to the cop who was watching things, and both of them moved in on Evan. Blair sat at the table across from him while the other cop took Adrian to one side, just out of earshot.

Blair spoke to Evan for several minutes. Evan could only shake his head mechanically to the gentle questions. In his bright and totally ridiculous clothes he looked like a sad-faced clown left stranded by his circus. Blair gave up for the time being and crossed to Adrian to hear his brief version of events, then it was our turn.

Unasked, Escott slipped quietly away and Blair took his place in our corner. We went through it all again, but no amount of talk could change the facts or soften them. He was interested in Evan's connection with Dimmy Wallace and the scuffle Adrian and I had with his stooges. He noted it all down, but kept his conclusions to himself.

Bobbi asked to be excused and disappeared into the bathroom. It was more diplomacy than body need or wanting to repair her makeup. She knew I could get more out of Blair alone and I silently blessed her brains and tact.

Blair followed her departure and turned his attention back to me. "Bad business, her getting involved in another murder so close to the one during her radio broadcast. And before that, it was those two at the Nightcrawler Club. Death seems to follow that young woman."

"That's why I'd like to keep this short, I want to take her home as soon as I can."

"Of course. Now, what can you tell me?" He put on the kind of manner that invites confidences, but I wasn't having any because I'd already told him everything.

"You know as much as I do, Lieutenant. I only met this bunch a couple of days ago. God knows I want to help, but I really can't add anything more."

"What about the names of their other friends at this party? They might provide us with more information on the Robleys' personal lives."

"There's Reva Stokes and Leighton Brett. There's also a tough named Dreyer who was at the party. He took a few swings at Evan over a crap game . . ."

We went around on the business for a while until I was repeating myself. Unlike our last meeting I was trying to cooperate, as this time I had nothing to hide.

"What now?" I asked when he looked ready to end the interview.

"Now we try and get Mr. Robley upstairs to see if anything was stolen."

"In his condition?"

"We haven't much of a choice. You only just met him and Mr. Adrian has stated he hasn't been here in some months. We just want him to take a quick look. If there was a robbery it will affect our investigation."

From that angle I could see the sense of it, but before he could start, another uniform came in and whispered in his ear. I heard it quite clearly but pretended not to. Blair looked at me, cocking his head slightly.

"Well, you speak of the devil and watch what happens. Miss Smythe's been making some phone calls."

Bobbi had long since emerged from the bathroom and was standing protectively close to Evan. "I felt I had to. They *are* friends of the family."

"That's all right," he assured. "I'm glad you did." He sent the cop off and a moment later Reva Stokes and Leighton Brett walked tentatively in. Reva looked shaken and was very white except for the red rims of her eyes, and she was hanging on to her fiancé like a lifeline. Brett had his arm around her and simply looked grim. Bobbi went to them and spoke in discreet tones, gesturing to Evan in explanation. Reva shook her head—in sadness, not refusal—found some strength within herself, and went over to take Evan's hand.

At this touch, he slowly raised his lost eyes. The muscles under his skin twitched a little, and he seemed ready to cry as he looked at her. I was hoping he would. He needed some kind of release; his blank silence was much more disturbing than Adrian's.

I glanced around for him, but at some point he'd left the room.

Blair introduced himself to Brett and explained the need for Evan to go up and see if anything was missing.

"The man hardly knows where he is, how can you expect him to help you?"

Diplomacy came easy for Blair, but then he was used to

handling all kinds of belligerents in his job, and Leighton Brett was just another voice in the crowd. "He's the only one who can do it. I would appreciate your help." He was polite, but there was an edge to his voice even Brett could not ignore. Growling and sullen, he went to Reva and told her what was wanted.

As though acting as translator, Reva spoke to Evan and somehow broke through the fog that was holding him. He nodded listlessly and the chair scraped over the faded linoleum as he found his feet. Blair proceeded and said nothing as Brett and I followed the slow parade upstairs.

A chalk outline and a little blood on the floor were the only indications of what all the fuss was about, unless you wanted to count the fingerprint dust everywhere. Evan identified Sandra's purse and nodded to confirm that the smaller change purse that would have carried her money was gone.

"Two dollars," he said clearly.

"What about two dollars?" asked Blair.

Evan searched his mind for the answer. "She doesn't carry more than two dollars. We don't have much, you see—"

"Is anything else missing? Did you keep any money or valuables?"

"We don't have much, you see." Evan was drifting again. He wandered around the room, blinking at the familiar now become horrible and unable to absorb the change. "You see . . ." He stared at the stacks of oil paintings in their storage slots against the wall.

Brett bulled his way past the cop at the door. "That's enough, the man needs a doctor, not pointless questions. If you're through—"

"Yes, I'm through, get him out of here."

Evan was now looking at the outline on the floor, a place we had all carefully stepped around. He was breathing faster, the air chopping in and out of his lungs in silent gusts. His mouth sagged shapelessly and a line of spittle spilled over the right corner in a fine thread. He began that terrible keening again, hopeless and frightening to hear.

Brett stepped forward to take his arm and the smaller man shook him off with unexpected strength. He rocked slightly from the waist, as though from cramp, and the keening grew louder.

The uniform next to me was gaping. He was young and had never seen anything like it before. I nudged him out of the spell. "You got a doctor here?"

His attention shifted reluctantly. "Yeah, maybe he's still—"

"Then go get him and make sure he's got his bag. *Move.*"

He moved, clattering down in his regulation shoes.

Brett tried to guide Evan out again, talking to him in a low voice. Evan stayed rooted to his spot and shook him off again. I stepped forward and motioned Brett to keep back. I looked into Evan's straining face, but couldn't quite reach his eyes. He wasn't seeing me or anything else in the room but the pathetic marks on the floor where his sister had fallen and left him forever.

I called his name, loudly. He matched it with more sound, which was beginning to rise into a full scream. I tried to focus onto him, but it was like squeezing quicksilver, he just wasn't there. He was lost in a place I could not follow. Sending men into madness is one thing, bringing them out of it was another and beyond even my powers at the moment.

Evan's scream died away for want of breath. No one touched him. We were waiting for him to go berserk, for him to start breaking things up so he could be restrained, but nothing like that happened. We could do nothing but wait, and it seemed like forever before a thin man with a black bag appeared. No one needed to explain what was needed. He quickly dug into the bag and prepared a syringe.

"Blair, make sure he doesn't kill me," was all that he said. He approached Evan as though the man were an unexploded bomb.

We moved in a little closer as the doctor slid the shoulder of Evan's coat back and freed one arm. With a pair of scissors, he cut open a section of the shirtsleeve below the elbow, swabbed the bare skin with cotton, and sank the needle into the vein. Evan never knew he was there.

It must have been a pretty massive shot, for within a few minutes his staring eyes began to glaze over and his heart and breathing slowed. As the tension leached out of his muscles, it seemed to do the same for the rest of us and we all visibly relaxed to a certain degree.

The doctor put his stuff away. "He's going into the hospital, Lieutenant, at least for overnight observation."

"No objections," said Blair. He mopped at the sweat on his forehead with a silk handkerchief.

"My fianceé and I are his friends, we want to take care of him," Brett offered.

The doctor shook his head. "He needs professional help for now. You can check on him in the morning if you like."

Evan could have complained about being invisible again, because they were talking as though he weren't in the room. In a way, he wasn't."

The drug in his system took him a few steps further along to oblivion and he swayed a little. I got to him just in time and swept him up before he hit the floor. By now he was utterly limp, a deadweight in my arms as I carried him to his room and put him onto the bed. The coverings were still unfinished from Sally's interrupted housekeeping lesson. Only a few hours ago the world had been normal.

The doctor came in and took his pulse. "Help me with the blankets," he said. "I want to keep him warm."

I pulled the bedclothes out from one side and folded them over Evan, then added a crumpled quilt that had been thrown over a chair. "He gonna be all right?"

"He's got enough stuff in him to keep him out for some hours yet. Ask me then. Has he a relative or friend who can come with him to the hospital?"

Adrian, perhaps, if I could find him. He was in only slightly better emotional shape than Evan, but perhaps having something to do might help him. "I'll see."

Brett was trying unsuccessfully to pump Blair for information and barely concealed his annoyance at my interruption.

"I'm taking Miss Smythe home, lieutenant," I said.

"Right." He looked at the young cop and told him to clear me with the others, then returned his attention to Brett.

Bobbi had reheated the coffee and was pouring some for Reva when I came down. Both had heard the scream and both had questions on their faces. The answer seemed inadequate to the experience.

"He's going to the hospital," I told them. "I thought Alex would want to go along."

"I'll find him," Reva volunteered, and gave her hot cup to me.

I looked at it stupidly, wondering what to do. A faint smile ghosted over Bobbi's face and she took the cup back.

"Can we go home yet?" she asked.

"As far as I know. I want to talk to Charles."

"He can call you at my place."

It sounded good to me. I told the cop on duty where we were going and walked out into a blinding burst of light.

Reporters. Of course. The kid with the camera knocked out the used flashbulb, quickly replaced it, and yelled at me to look at him. I spun Bobbi around and hustled both of us back into the house.

"*Damn*. Where's the back way out of this dump?"

The cop pointed and we followed his direction, but two of them were waiting in the alley behind the house, kicking idly at the spillage from the garbage cans and smoking. It was a hell of a way to make a living and at the moment I was hard pressed to believe I'd been one of them only a month or so back.

"Let's just go on," said Bobbi.

But I dug in my heels, feeling the anger surfacing and badly needing to do something about it. "Wait here a minute, I'll take care of them."

She nodded and let me go out the battered screen door. They were on me like flies on fresh meat, shouting questions over each other and threatening to bring more people in with their noise. I held up a hand and achieved a pause in the barrage.

"Okay, fellas, one at a time." I pointed to the older one. "You first. Come over here so you can see what you're writing."

"That's fine, I just wanna know who's talking."

He backed me over to the door, where we could make use of the light from the house. His crony hung close enough to listen, his notepad ready and pencil poised over it. I ignored him and froze onto the older man's eyes.

"I want you to stand very still and not move for five minutes. You won't see or hear anything during that time and you won't remember me."

It helps when they're off guard. His partner's cigarette sagged in puzzlement, but it only lasted as long as it took for me to give him the same instructions. I went in for Bobbi and we walked past them, two improbable statues on display in a dank setting.

Bobbi was all wide-eyed. "They'll burn themselves—"

"Good point." I went back and thoughtfully removed the cigarettes from slack mouths, dropping them into a handy puddle.

"You . . . I mean, you hypnotized them?" she asked. "You *really* hypnotized them?"

"It comes with the condition."

"That's just like in that book."

"No, that's just like me."

"Do you do it a lot?"

"Not often."

"How do you do it?"

"Beats me. Watch where you step, sweetheart."

We picked our way out of the alley and came up to my car from behind. It was across the street from the house and as yet had not been noticed. I opened the door and slid across to the driver's side. By the time Bobbi was in I had the engine going and shifted it into first. We took the first corner right and headed for her hotel.

"Poor Sandra," she whispered. I only just heard her above the low rumble of the car. I took a hand off the wheel and covered hers briefly. It felt very small and cold.

"You want to stop somewhere for a drink?"

"No, I just want to be home. I want my own things around me."

It was a natural reaction to head for the safety of one's own nest. We said nothing for the rest of the trip. The silence held until I unlocked her door and turned on the living-room light. She was spooked and I obligingly checked all the rooms of her apartment before she took off her jacket and sat down. A brief raid on her liquor cabinet produced a medicinal shot of brandy, which she gratefully accepted.

"You all right?" she asked.

"I was wondering the same about you."

"I'm just scared and shaky."

"It'll pass."

She nodded absently and went into the kitchen to put her empty shot glass in the sink. When she came out she didn't settle back on the couch with me again, but wandered around the room touching and straightening things. Blair's words about death following her floated annoyingly through my mind.

She poked at some nonexistent dust on her Philco and rubbed her fingers clean. "I think I'll get out of this stuff and have a shower. Will you keep me company? Talk to me?"

"Anything you want."

I watched her take her clothes off, her movements unself-conscious and automatic. That fist gripped my gut again as I thought of the young girl I'd killed. She'd been the same way.

While the water hissed on the other side of the protective curtain we talked of God knows what, about anything except what had happened tonight. She shut the water off and I handed her a towel.

"I guess there is an advantage to short hair," she murmured, dabbing at the damp ends the shower spray had caught. She dried off and I helped her slip into her white satin robe. She tied off the belt and put her arms around me, resting her head on my chest. Her skin was warm and smelled pleasantly of soap. This lasted a minute and she broke away to go back to the living room.

She curled up on the couch, tucking her bare feet under the folds of the robe.

"Tell me what's on your mind," I said.

Her eyes dropped. "I'm trying not to think. It's what I feel and I feel guilty for feeling it."

I shoved some magazines to one side on the coffee table and sat on it to face her. "I know what it's like."

"I know you do. Were you scared when it happened?"

"What? Tonight?"

"No, back then . . . when . . . when they killed you."

This wasn't what I had expected.

"I'm scared, Jack. I'm scared of dying and I thought if you could tell me about it . . ."

She'd watched them carry Sandra out and had seen herself in that long basket.

"Tell me what scares you," I said.

"All of it. I'm afraid it might hurt or take days and days, but mostly that it won't make any difference, that I'll just not be here and no one will notice. I know you would, and Charles, and some of my friends, but the world will go on and I won't be here to see it. I don't want to be left behind. I don't want to leave you."

"You won't." But my heart was aching already. With care and caution I could live for centuries, but Bobbi . . . I shied away from that agonizing thought.

I moved to the couch and cuddled her into my arms. Maureen and I had faced the same decision, though the circumstances had been very different. I'd chosen out of love for her, not fear of my own mortality.

As though reading my thoughts, Bobbi said, "I love you, Jack. I can't bear the thought of leaving you. That's what scares me the most."

"What did you say?"

"I love you, I don't ever want to leave you." She turned to look up at me, her hazel eyes searching mine for a response. "The only other thing that scared me was telling you that, but after tonight I knew I had to."

"You were afraid of telling me . . ."

"It's an important word to me and everything that goes with it is frightening—at least for me."

That was true; it was frightening and exhilarating and the best and the worst all rolled together, and I'd been afraid to say it, too. We could go to bed and make love, but say nothing about it before, during or afterward. It was ridiculous.

"You don't have to be frightened," I said, my voice shaking. "At least you don't have to be frightened to love. . . ." And for the next few minutes everything got gloriously, radiantly incoherent.

* * *

Bobbi lay contentedly back in my arms, her breathing normal again, her eyes sleepy. "Are we awful?" she asked.

"How so?"

"To do this after poor Sandra—"

"It's normal. You get close to death and you want to reaffirm life. That's why a lot of babies are born during wars."

"What we do doesn't make babies."

"The instincts are still there, though."

"According to you it doesn't make vampires, either."

"Not unless we exchanged blood. Your famous book at least got that right."

"Stop picking on my book."

"Okay."

She was waking up a little, one hand stroking the spot on the vein under her jaw where I'd gone in. "That's been on my mind, you know."

"Exchanging?"

"We talked about it before."

"I remember." We'd talked about it, but not nearly enough. It was a hard subject for me to open up on.

"You said that's what Gaylen wanted, but you didn't want to give it to her."

"She was insane. It didn't show, but part of me must have known. That's why I didn't want to do it."

"What about to me?"

"How do you feel about it?"

She shrugged. "I don't think I know enough yet to tell you."

"That's a good answer."

"It's not easy for you, is it?"

I drew a breath and sighed. "It's just at times all I see are the disadvantages. My life is limited in a lot of ways, ways I'd never thought about until it was too late."

"Like what?"

"For one thing, I miss socializing over food, and I'm really beginning to hate mirrors. Sunlight blinds and paralyzes me, and if I don't sleep on my earth I have the most god-awful dreams. Going to the Stockyards is a real pain. I often leave it till late so I don't have the cattle smell on me all the evening and can wash it off when I get home."

"Did she feel the same way?" She was referring to Maureen.

"She let me know what to expect, but she never complained, except about mirrors whenever she bought new clothes." But Maureen had had decades to adjust to things and I was still grass green. Maybe in time . . .

"Then why did you want to change?"

"I loved her."

"Don't you believe I love you just as much?"

"Yes. I see what you're getting at, Bobbi, but you need to know there are no guarantees. We could do it, but it might not work."

"And then again, it might. I don't see it as a promise or even as insurance, but it *is* hope. That's all I really want, Jack, just that piece of hope."

I thought long and hard about it for maybe two seconds. She had a serious decision ahead, though I was sure she'd made up her mind already. When I'd talked things out with Maureen, I'd been the same. I'd loved her and we both wanted the hope in the background of our lives that it would continue. Now I loved Bobbi and life was repeating itself.

"Look, you need to see exactly what it's like for me. I want you to know the worst of it, and then if you still feel the same—"

"What are you talking about?"

"I want to take you to the Stockyards. I think you need to see what it is that I have to do every few nights."

"You want to show me how you eat?"

Things twisted inside. "I don't eat, Bobbi. I open up a vein in a live animal with my teeth and drink its blood."

She shifted around a little and crossed her arms, prepared for hostilities. "Are you trying to put me off?"

"I'm trying to give you an idea of what it's like to live this way."

"And painting anything but a rosy picture about it. Don't you think you're being too hard on yourself?"

"Well, I—"

"And passing that attitude on to me is hardly fair to either of us."

"Uh . . ."

"Exactly," she said. "Now, how about some straight honesty? Is what you do really so horrible? What happens to the cow after you're through with it?"

"Well, nothing. I don't drain them dry, you know."

"I didn't know, but I'm not too surprised or you'd have to have a hollow leg. As for the cow, she hangs around in a smelly pen until driven to the slaughterhouse, then some guy smacks her between the eyes with a sledgehammer. Depending on how she's processed, sooner or later she ends up on my dinner table. Does that make me better than you just because I pay to have someone else do the dirty work?"

I'd thought the whole business out before, but had never applied such logic specifically to Bobbi. She had me cold and she knew it. She smiled as the dawning finally broke on me.

Somehow things didn't seem so hard, after all.

$$\begin{array}{c} \blacktriangle \\ 8 \\ \blacktriangledown \end{array}$$

WE SPENT A little more time talking and decided to postpone our Stockyards visit for some other night. Bobbi was physically and emotionally exhausted and I wanted her to sleep on things. My own trip there could not be put off, though. I was getting nerved up and had to concentrate on simple tasks—indications that I badly needed my long drink. After seeing her to bed, I drove straight over.

I'd purposefully overfed last time and it had bought me an extra hunger-free night. The tiny amounts I took from Bobbi also helped to some degree, but were really insufficient to maintain me. Earlier, when my lips were on her throat, it had taken a conscious effort on my part not to go in a little deeper. The temptation had certainly been present, and this time it had been very difficult to end things and pull away. When hungry, my body only knew that blood was blood, whether acquired by feeding off cattle or through sex with Bobbi. The very real possibility existed that I might lose control and continue taking from her past the point of safety. To prevent that, I wanted to be well supplied from a less fragile, more bountiful source.

Again, I parked on a different street from my last visit, ghosted in, and did what I had to do. Bobbi's logic floated through my mind as I knelt and drank. Talking things over with her made one hell of a difference; tonight was the first time I admitted to myself that I enjoyed the taste of the animal's blood. It *is* different from human blood, like the difference between milk and champagne: one nourishes and the other leaves you high as a kite. Tonight I'd had the best of both.

The feeling lasted until I was back on the street again and walking to my car. I was walking, seeing things, thinking thoughts, and Sandra Robley was dead, her inert body awaiting its turn for the autopsy table. Some *bastard* had shut her down. God knows why; there's never a good reason to be a victim.

I got in and drove half a block on an impulse. It paid off. The lights of Escott's second-floor office were glowing. Parked near his door, just behind his own huge Nash, was one of the newer Lincolns. It was really too late for him to be interviewing clients, so his visitor was probably connected with the murder investigation in some way. I shut down my motor and softly approached the building. Beneath his window, open to catch the night breeze, I could listen in on their conversation.

". . . anything, absolutely anything at all, I would be very grateful to know about it."

"Do you wish to retain my services, then?" Escott asked.

"Inasmuch as you are connected with this . . . this terrible business."

A drawer slid open. "Very well. Here is my standard contract. It's fairly straightforward. I cannot make you any promises, and in a case such as this I am under strict limitations. If I should find evidence pointing to a specific person's guilt I am legally bound to turn it immediately over to the police." He sounded extremely formal and was uncharacteristically discouraging, an indication he was not happy with his latest employer.

"You mean you think Alex did it?"

"I have no opinion one way or another, I merely follow a line of inquiry until all questions are answered."

I lost the reply, because by then I was walking up the covered stairs to the office. Two raps on the frosted glass of the outer door seemed sufficient to announce me, and I was inside, matching interested looks with Leighton Brett. His big frame and expensive clothes made him look out of place in the institutional wood chair opposite Escott's equally plain desk.

He was puzzled by my showing up, but it shifted into

acceptance when Escott greeted me and explained I was an associate.

"I thought you were a writer," said Brett, turning it into a friendly jibe.

"Only on my days off. This is what puts bacon on the table."

"Mr. Fleming was the one who originally called me in," said Escott.

"I'm glad he did, you were the only one there talking any sense."

It seemed more likely that Escott had been the only one there willing to listen to him.

"How did things wind up?" I asked. There was no other place to sit so I hitched a leg over one corner of the desk.

Escott moved a heavy glass ashtray a little to give me more room. It contained only one dead cigarette and no pipe dottles. They hadn't been there long. "Evan Robley is in the hospital—Miss Stokes is sitting with him now—and Alex Adrian has gone missing."

"What do you mean? Is he out on a drunk or just not home?"

"The police are waiting for him to turn up at his residence."

"To arrest him?"

"Possibly. Lieutenant Blair is being especially close about his plans, but Adrian's disappearance from the crime scene does not look good."

"It stinks to high heaven, Charles, and we all know it." I turned to Brett. "You know him best, where would he be?"

He spread his large hands. "I haven't had much contact with him since Celia died. Evan might know, but with the condition he's in . . ." He didn't have to finish, but thinking about Evan gave him another idea. "I could call Reva at the hospital, she and Sandra . . ." Again, he did not finish.

Escott pushed his desk phone toward him and we waited as he went through the motions. While he struggled to locate Evan's hospital room and consequently his fiancée I quietly asked for more information.

"What did you get from the other tenants?"

"The people on the same floor were out all evening. Those above did hear a man and woman arguing, thought nothing of it, and turned their radio up to drown the noise. The rest were a singularly deaf and incurious lot with problems of their own. A quarreling couple is not an oddity in that neighborhood."

"And nothing on who the man was or what the fight was about?"

"Nothing at all. No one is even sure if the argument is even connected with the crime; it could have been quite another couple fighting."

"What do you think?"

"That I need more information. There was one thing which you might enlighten me about: one of the reporters there was asking after you by name."

Oh yeah?

"Extremely female, tall, with dark hair and light brown eyes; very well dressed and quite striking."

"Barb Steler."

"The journalist who knew Adrian in Paris?"

"The same. Wonder what she wanted."

"An interview?"

"No, thanks. As it was, Bobbi and I barely made it out of there. She probably spotted me when that photographer popped a flash right in my kisser."

"I wonder if you left an image on the negative," he mused in a very low voice so Brett wouldn't hear.

"I hope not. The last thing I want is my mug plastered all over the morning editions."

Brett hung up and shook his head at us. "Sorry, but she said she couldn't think of anyone or any place Alex would go to. She's hoping he'll turn up at the hospital to check on Evan."

"If he left prior to Mr. Robley's breakdown, he won't know to go there," Escott pointed out.

"Yes. *Damn*, how could he go tearing off like this?" Brett smacked the desk lightly with the flat of his hand, then got to his feet. "I have to leave now, Reva made it clear she doesn't want to be alone anymore."

"Of course, and if I should learn anything . . ."

It reminded Brett of the business contract on the blotter. "I think I'll take this along for reading material. You'll hear from me in the morning."

We all said good night and Escott let him out the door. He

didn't speak again until Brett's Lincoln rolled off and cleared the street.

"You've an idea?" He made it more statement than question.

"Just a small one. This assumes that Alex didn't kill her and that before he disappeared he was able to get some kind of sense out of Evan."

"Concerning Dimmy Wallace?"

"Jeez, Charles, why do I bother to think with you around?"

He took it as a compliment. "Our problem is to locate Wallace."

"No problem," I told him.

A smile briefly crossed his bony face as he understood the reference. "My phone is entirely at your disposal."

I entirely made use of it. The call took almost as long as Brett's, but I finally got through to Gordy.

"This is Fleming. I need an address."

There was a pause, because Gordy survived through caution. "Whose?"

"Dimmy Wallace."

"He making trouble again?"

"No, but I'm trying to prevent it. Someone I know might be gunning for him. I want to stop it."

A longer pause, but I knew Gordy wasn't one to waste words or time. The line was empty for a few seconds, then he came back with an address, which I wrote down. "You never called me for this, got it?"

"I never even heard of you—and thanks." I hung up and turned to Escott. "He says it's an all-night gas station."

He glanced at my scribble. "It's on the south side—enemy territory for our benefactor, if I recall the current gang political situation correctly. His wish for anonymity is well placed."

"Wallace isn't there all the time, he's usually on the move, but we might be able to talk to the people there."

"Most assuredly *you* will be able to communicate with them. Please allow me a moment to prepare before we leave, though." He opened the door behind his desk and made use of the inner room it served. There he kept an old army cot and some spare clothing, among other things. When he finally emerged, he looked slightly heavier and sported an unmistakable bulge beneath his coat under the right arm.

"Ready?" I asked.

"As I shall ever be. We'll take my car."

And no chances; he wanted his bulletproof vest, gun, and the armor plating of the Nash between himself and the unknowns that Dimmy Wallace represented. I approved. Chicago could play indecently rough at times.

Escott handled his big tank of a car, along with its extra weight in steel, the way Astaire danced with Rogers. He very obviously derived a lot of pleasure from driving and my guess was that if he loved anything, he loved his Nash, bullet dimples in the doors and all.

We were up to the speed limit, but he didn't seem to be in a hurry to arrive. That kind of urgency was missing from his attitude. We took a few turnings and though my knowledge of the city was still sketchy, I knew we weren't on a direct route to the south side.

"What's up, Charles?"

"Someone is following us," he said with quiet interest.

The hard blue glare of the streetlights struck his chest, traveled up to his chin and vanished as our car moved forward. It reminded me that whoever was behind us would see my outline if I turned around to look, so I didn't.

"Can you tell who they are?"

"Unfortunately, no. Their headlights are in the way."

"What d'you want to do about it?"

"There are a number of options open to us."

"I'm all ears."

His eyes flicked up to the rearview mirror, then back to the road. "I can lose them . . ."

"Aren't we a little too big for that?"

"Shoe Coldfield did somewhat more than add special glass and armoring when he owned this particular vehicle. There were some slight modifications to improve engine efficiency as well."

"Why is it that I'm not very surprised?"

"Haven't the faintest. Now the problem with losing them is

that we may never know who they are, and such antics are
liable to arouse the curiosity of the local constabulary."

"What other options have you got?"

"We can pretend to be unaware of them and lead them to a
spot convenient to us, and—as it is so colorfully put in
westerns—get the drop on them."

"I like that one. Got any particular spot in mind?"

"Yes, I'm heading for it now."

"Had it all worked out beforehand?"

"More or less, but it seemed best to keep moving until I'd
discussed things with you. I'm so glad our decisions are in
accordance."

"What if they weren't?"

"I'm not sure, but since they are, it hardly seems relevant to
speculate over might-have-beens."

That was true. I was just nervous and he was being polite
and not pointing it out to me—not in so many words. Escott
ought to have been the nervous one, as he was physically far
more vulnerable than I, but he liked this kind of work. He
seemed to feed off tension the way I fed off cattle.

"I plan to rely on your speed and other special abilities," he
told me.

"Okay."

"I'm going to take a turn into an alley ahead and go slow
enough for you to get out. When the other car comes through,
I'll have stopped at the far end. Chances are they will also stop,
and you can improvise from there."

"And if they don't follow you in?"

"Then we'll go to plan B."

"Which is . . . ?"

"I'll let you know when I think of it."

I shook my head, but it didn't matter much. If this stunt
didn't come off no doubt he *would* think of something else.

He made a leisurely turn into a narrow space between two
long buildings. Dark walls of brick and useless, soot-stained
windows slipped past and slowed as he took his foot from the
gas and shifted gears. There was enough room to open the
door, but I didn't bother. When we were down to ten miles an
hour I dematerialized and slipped out.

Smack in front of me was the solidity of the right-hand building, which I used to orient myself. Turning and pressing my back (such as it was in this state) to the wall, I very slowly eased into the world again, but only a little. I was mostly transparent, which meant that unless I moved around or lost concentration and went whole, the party in the other car couldn't easily see me. On the other hand, I could still get a very good look at them.

Their headlights were dark as they turned into the alley. They saw Escott's car far ahead of them, but slowed to think things over. It gave me a good chance to identify the driver.

Escott had said to improvise, right now I was torn between anger and curiosity. When the first wave of it passed, they were halfway to me. I could wait for them, rush in, and do my Lamont Cranston imitation, or I could find Escott again and tell him to get us lost. Both were equally tempting.

Now they were within ten feet of me and sailing slowly past, so I made a decision, materialized, grabbed the passenger-door handle, and yanked it open.

In the crowded confusion of the front seat of the car, I wasn't sure who screamed the loudest at my sudden appearance: the young photographer clutching his camera or Barbara Steler clutching the steering wheel.

Out of reflex, she hit the brakes and the engine stalled. The kid with the camera made an abortive attempt to push me out, but I got my left arm inside in time and pushed him against the seat hard enough for him to lose his breath. The arm remained, to hold him up and to give him something to think about.

Barbara tried the starter, but their car was flooded now. She looked up—fear flashed through those huge bronze eyes for a second until she recognized me—then she slammed her hands on the steering wheel.

"*Damn* it! Where in *hell* did you come from?"

I'd meant to give them a good scare and couldn't keep the grin off my face. "Ask my mother, she knows all about it."

"You never had one, you bastard."

"Temper, temper. Maybe you'd like to tell me why you're following us around."

"You used to be in the business. Work it out." She put a

palm to her forehead and tried to slow her breathing. The adrenaline surge caused by my entrance had them both shaking.

"Barb . . ." this from the photographer, in a slightly strangled tone. My arm had slid up to his neck. I eased the pressure but kept the same position.

She saw what had happened and suddenly threw her head back and laughed. The kid joined in, but not too enthusiastically. When she recovered, her body was less tense and she had an air of being in charge of things. She opened her door and got out, walking around to wait in front of the car. I told the kid to stay put. He was still wobbly and content to do as he was told without any special influence on my part.

Barbara was in somber black, right down to her kid gloves and silk stockings. It brought out the ivory of her skin and made me want to see more of it than was decently possible under any circumstances. Her full lips were softly curved into the kind of smile a woman gets when she correctly reads a man's mind.

"This is hardly the perfect place to talk," she began.

"Good, because you won't be getting any interviews."

"Darling Jack, don't be offended, but I don't want to interview you, I just want you to help me arrange one."

The endearment was interesting, considering what hadn't happened during our last encounter. "Who did you have in mind?"

"Alex Adrian, of course."

"And you think I know where he is?"

"Or your friend, Mr. Escott. He must be getting impatient waiting for you down there." She indicated the far end of the alley. "Why don't you run along to him and continue on your errand?"

"Only if you back out and go home."

"But it's such a long drive from here, I couldn't possibly return empty handed."

"Force yourself."

"My dear, you of all people should know I *never* force myself."

The alley suddenly felt very close and warm. "Yes, well, there's a first time for everything, Barbara—"

"I mean it, Jack, I want to see Alex." Her manner shifted to a more serious tone and I wondered if she were lying again. This time I couldn't tell.

"Why?"

"Because the police are after him for walking out on the scene of a murder. I talked with them. He's in very serious trouble. He needs help—" She stopped and straightened, as though she's said too much for her own comfort and regretted the words.

"You still love him?"

She wasn't happy that I knew that and her eyes flared, then shifted away. "Think what you like, but please take me along."

"Women who love Alex always seem to come to a bad end. Are you sure—"

She moved as fast as a striking snake, her palm cracking sharp and loud. Outrage rolled from her like a wave, more tangible to me than the slap. She looked ready to add a verbal insult to the injury but was too mad to think of one acid enough to suit the occasion.

"I guess you're sure," I said, rubbing where she'd hit my cheek. It hadn't hurt.

She turned on her heel to go back to her car.

"Barbara, wait a minute."

"No."

"I'm sorry I said that, but I had to know where you really stand."

She paused at the door. "I'll find him myself."

"Not alone, you won't."

"How else, then, if you—"

"Maybe I will help you."

That stopped her cold.

"I'll talk to my partner."

It was my turn to walk away and I felt her eyes on my back all down the length of the alley. Escott had the motor running, ready for us to bolt if necessary. He shut it down when I came up on the driver's side and started talking. He wasn't happy about my request.

"I'm reluctant to involve anyone else in this, especially a member of the fourth estate."

"She wants to come for her own reasons. Her paper has second place this time."

"I understand that, but are her personal motives going to get in the way of things? I've no wish to expose anyone to unnecessary risk."

"She could also act as backup for us. She can drive and be safe enough in your car. That sporter they're in wouldn't hold up to a good rainstorm."

"A good point, but are you sure you couldn't tell her to go home?"

"I could, but I don't want to."

"Is she immune or something?"

"No, I just want her along."

Humor and frustration mixed in his expression and then vanished with a shrug. "Very well, but no photographer. That's the prerequisite I place upon her coming with us."

I ducked out before he could change his mind.

Barbara accepted the offer with ill-concealed astonishment. "Why—I mean—after I—oh, never mind, we'll be right behind you."

"Hold on, Charles said only you could come, so don't insist on having a saddle with your gift horse."

She looked ready to contend the point and visibly worked to change her mind. It took a little more than logic to talk the kid into it, though. He was anything but crazy about letting her run off to parts unknown with two strangers; that was his main argument. Unspoken was the simple fact that he didn't want to be left out. Barb smiled, though, ran a well-calculated finger down the side of his face, and all his determination melted into an ineffectual puddle in less than a second. He took over the driver's side and solemnly promised to take the car back to the newspaper offices for her.

She kissed her fingertip and tapped it on his nose, and that made his whole week. Then I stepped in and caught his attention. I didn't do much more than repeat his promise back to him, but from the slackening of his expression I knew for certain he'd keep it.

"My, but you're suspicious," she commented as we watched him back the car out of the narrow space. "Did you think he doesn't understand plain English?"

"Like you reminded me, I used to be in the business. Neither of us would want a breach of trust at this point, would we?"

"Darling, it's the farthest thing from my mind."

"Good. Keep it there."

She slipped a friendly arm into mine as we walked up to Escott, who got out to meet us. When I introduced them, she flashed him the kind of smile that could knock over a bank vault. They exchanged pleasantries as though we were at some fancy tea party and not a dank alley just off the river with God knows what lurking around the next corner. Escott was apparently not immune to the charm of someone he'd described as "extremely female."

"We must have some ground rules," he said, finally bringing up business. "It is not likely we'll even find anything tonight, but if we do, you follow our orders."

She murmured agreement, maybe a little too readily for my peace of mind, but if it became necessary, I could enforce things as I did with the photographer.

He held the door for her and she stepped into the backseat like a queen going on a tour. "Lock the doors and if we tell you to duck, don't ignore it," he suggested.

Something in his tone got her attention and she banked the charm down for the time being and nodded seriously.

I got in, Escott got in, and we moved back out onto the street. He put a few extra turns in our route south, just to make sure no other cars had been waiting for us. None were, so he made a beeline to the address.

The gas station we wanted was a solid-looking cinder-block structure sloppily coated with dirty white paint. It sported two battered pumps out front and a garage on the left of a tiny office. Parked in front of the garage door was a well-dented open-bed truck. The fenced back area contained a broken-down carriage, dozens of rusting fifty-gallon drums, and stacks of balding tires. It wasn't the kind of place a mother would take her kid to for a rest stop.

Escott pulled in and we waited for someone to emerge and

sell us some gas. I got out to do what I hoped was a passable imitation of a man stretching his legs. Barbara remained quietly where she was, her big eyes wide open and watchful.

A cadaverous old man with half a cigarette growing from the corner of his mouth squinted at us from his sanctum by the cash box, deciding if it were worth his while to leave it. He finally concluded we were staying and levered to his feet. As he drifted past, I could almost hear the pop and creak of his joints. He leaned into the driver's window and muttered something in a rusty-saw voice that might have been a question. Escott apparently had a gift for translating obscure dialects and asked for a few gallons of gas. The old man hawked and spat—without losing his dead cigarette—and did things with one of the pumps.

He kept a cold eye on me as I wandered around. A suspicious person might think I had designs on the cash box, so I avoided the front office, if not the suspicion. The garage part was closed off, but something about it had my attention on a gut level and I moved closer to listen.

The wide door had two filthy windows. They were dark, but only because of the black paint smeared on the interior side of the glass. Maybe the station owner had a legitimate reason for such aggressive privacy. Maybe.

I moved along the front of the garage with my ears flapping, but between the wind stirring things around and the gas pumping away I couldn't pick up anything on the inside. Escott was trying a little friendly conversation with the old man and kept him busy checking the oil and cleaning windows. While they investigated something or other under the hood, I went around the corner and pressed an ear against the building.

What I got for my trouble was a dirty ear. If there were any people inside, they were so quiet about it that I'd have to go in to find out.

Brick walls are no real trouble for me—I'd found that out the first time I discovered how to vanish—but filtering through one like coffee in a percolator was not my idea of fun. High up, just below the roof overhang, was a long row of fly-specked windows. It would be easier to slip through any existing gaps in their casements; they'd be small, but better than the wall.

Once I'd gone transparent and floated up, I could see from all the rust that they hadn't been opened in years, and the corner of one of the panes was beautifully broken away. Grateful at this piece of luck, I disappeared completely and slipped through the three-inch opening like sand in an hourglass.

My hearing wasn't much better inside than out, though I thought I heard some kind of scraping sound. In my immediate area I was lodged between the wall and a series of thick surfaces curving away from me that I couldn't identify. The ceiling was only inches above, and down where my feet would be I couldn't feel anything but air. I hate heights.

Then I definitely heard voices and forgot about mental discomforts.

"Lay that off, you dummy."

"But it's gettin' thick."

"So put in more water."

The scraping stopped. "Why don't he get rid of 'em?"

"Shuddup."

It was like trying to listen through a load of blankets. One cautious degree at a time I sieved back into the real world, just enough to hear and see and hopefully not be seen. The curved things turned out to be a rack of old tires and I was hovering between them and the wall. The more solid I became, the heavier I got, and it took no small effort to maintain my half-transparent state. Being fifteen feet over a cement floor without any other support than air and willpower did not help my concentration.

The garage had two doors; the big one in the front for the cars and a regular one that served the office. The remaining three walls were lined with rows of tires, and below these were greasy workbenches and a confused scattering of tools and supplies. A man had the office door open a crack and was keeping an eye on the outside. His back was to me, but I was sure I didn't know him. He wore a dark purple suit with orange pinstripes, and nobody I knew outside of a circus would have been caught dead in such a getup.

Standing just behind him, trying unsuccessfully to look over his shoulder, was Francis Koller. Since the other man was bigger, Francis gave up and went back to stirring a shovel around a large, flat container shaped like a shallow horse trough. He was trying to be quiet about it, but the shovel would sometimes go its own way and scrape along the bottom. The viscous, cold-looking gray stuff in the trough was cement.

"I said to lay off," the other man hissed, not turning around. Francis laid off.

"Where the hell is the other bozo?" he griped.

Francis deduced it to be a rhetorical question and didn't bother to answer.

The other bozo had to be a reference to myself. Until I returned to Escott's car, whatever they were up to would have to wait, but Escott would be running out of stalls by this point. There were only so many he could try before they became too obvious.

I shifted a little, taking care not to bump the tires. My view of the garage widened.

The center of the floor was broken up by the grease pit, its wide rectangular opening covered by a metal grid. Standing against the opposite wall were a half dozen rusting fifty-gallon drums with various faded labels on them. One of them had been pulled out from the rest and its cover removed. It was positioned exactly under a heavy-duty block-and-tackle arrangement used to lift motors out of cars. A thick, taut chain ran from the supporting framework above down to a steel hook. Attached to the hook was a knotting of rope and hanging from the rope by his wrists was Alex Adrian.

His slack figure was motionless and his head drooped down on his chest. I couldn't see his face. The toes of his shoes dangled just over the open mouth of the metal drum. Enlightenment came with a fast and sickening twist of the gut. I suddenly knew what they were going to do with all the cement.

9

THE AIR WAS foul from the stink of spilled gas by the car. When I materialized I had to steady myself against one of the pumps because the sickness had followed me from the garage.

At that distance I couldn't tell if he was alive or dead. If dead, then we could take our time; if alive, then we had none left to spare. And if they put him alive into that drum . . .

With the pumps and car between us I knew the man watching from the station couldn't see me, and no one had noticed my return. Escott and the old man were still poking at things under the hood and Barb was watching the spot where I'd gone around the far corner of the garage. I tapped on her window. She whirled and slid over to roll it open.

"What's the matter?" she whispered, too worried to question how I'd gotten there. "Did you find anything?"

I could only nod and realized it would not be wise to get too detailed. "They've got Alex. They're—"

"Is he all right?"

"I don't know, I couldn't see that much. There're two men inside, and they've got him trussed like a turkey." She made to move and I stopped it with a short, hard gesture. *"Don't,* they're watching us right now. They're only waiting for us to leave—"

"But we can't—"

"Yes, we will. You and Charles are going to drive off and

find the nearest phone. You call the cops and get them here as
fast as you can."

"What about you?"

"I'm staying here to keep an eye on them."

She dived into her purse and brought out a beautiful
nickel-and-mother-of-pearl derringer, pushing it into my hand.
"Here, you'll have two shots. You have to remember to cock
it first before pulling the trigger . . . you *do* know how to
shoot?"

"Yeah, but—"

"Just in case," she said, and I knew it would be easier to
pocket the thing than argue with her.

"Okay, thanks. You get the cops here fast, got it?"

"Yes—"

"And an ambulance, too."

"Ambulance?" The word moved on her lips with no sound
behind it.

"Just in case." Adrian might need it if he was still alive, and
if not, then his killers most certainly would before I was
finished. "Has Charles mentioned me at all while he's been
keeping Chuckles busy?"

Her expression flickered as she shifted thoughts and tried to
remember. "I don't think so, he's been talking about the car the
whole time. Why?"

"You'll see." I hoped Escott would follow my lead.

The old man glared at the engine with contempt and shook
his head at Escott's latest question. "I jus' pump the gas, I'm
tellin' you I don't know nuthin' 'bout these things."

"But just listening does not require any mechanical skill,
and I'm sure if you did so while I pressed the accelerator, you'd
be able to hear it as well." Escott was using his most persuasive
voice and sounded like an amiable idiot. He looked up as I
approached. "Oh, hello, I was trying—"

"Just wanted to say thanks for the lift," I interrupted,
holding out my hand. He'd picked up the cue without batting
an eye and we shook briefly.

"You're not coming along?" he asked.

"No, this is where I get off. I already said good-bye to your
missus. See you around."

He wished me well and continued to argue happily with the old man for another few minutes, long enough for me to take to the sidewalk and stroll away out of sight. I blessed the actor in him, vanished again, and doubled back.

The sidewalk was my prime landmark. I followed its flat, hard surface, keeping low out of instinct rather than necessity. In this form, body posture is meaningless, but the illusion of it in the mind is a comfort.

My second landmark was the old truck parked in front of the garage door, where I turned left, moving forward until I felt the wall of the garage itself. Floating upward, I quickly found the window with the broken pane. The last faint outside noise I heard was Escott's Nash starting up. Pouring inside to the spot behind the tires, I faded enough of myself back into the world to see and hear things.

They hadn't moved. Francis held his shovel in the trough of cement, the man at the door kept watch, and Adrian hung motionless from the ropes. After stuffing him into the oil drum and filling the leftover spaces up with cement, they'd probably load it onto the back of their truck. North of us was a perfectly good lake with miles of coastline; finding a deserted spot to dump their problem wouldn't be too hard.

"You took your time," the man complained, holding the door for the old geezer to come in.

"They din' wanna leave and so what? He's gone now."

"What about that other one? Where'd he go?"

"Off. Hitchin' a ride and got hisself unhitched."

"You sure?"

"I seen him walk."

Francis resumed scraping at the cement. "This shit's starting to set, Dimmy, we gotta *move*."

"Who's stopping you?" he snarled back.

Dimmy Wallace: bookie, loan shark, and new terror of the south side, but then Francis was easily impressed. I saw a middle-size, stocky man who badly needed to cut the limp blond hair straggling from under his hat. He had a pudgy face and colorless eyes with the kind of blank expression you usually find on infants or lunatics.

Francis took the hint with a short, relishing laugh and put

down his shovel. "C'mere, Pops, gimme a hand." He went to a length of chain leading down from the pulley mechanism above, presumably so he could lower Adrian down into the oil barrel.

Pops thought it over sourly. "Nuh-uh. None o' this crap, I pump gas."

"I said I need a hand," Francis insisted, but apparently he was too much a junior member of the team to swing any authority. Pops turned around and went back to the tiny office. Francis tossed a comment about the old man's ancestry to his indifferent back and unhooked the chain from the wall in disgust.

Bringing Adrian's body down a few more feet was a strain for him. Dimmy Wallace made no move to help, nor was he asked. When Adrian started to double over, Francis reversed the chain to take in the slack. He strutted up, hands on his hips, the owner of a brand-new toy.

"Do I kill him now or wait and watch him squeal?" he asked Wallace.

That was the best news I'd heard all evening. It gave me a whole new set of worries, but at least I knew Adrian was alive.

"Do what you want, but just do it. We ain't got all night." Wallace was bored with the business.

"We got till Toumey comes back."

"You got till the cement sets. Remember?"

Francis did, much to his disgust. He wasted no more time and poked at Adrian's downturned face. "Hey, Mr. Hot Shit. C'mon, you don't wanna miss any of this."

"Give 'im some air," Wallace suggested.

Francis moved faster than thought. A knife appeared like magic in his hand and the blade slashed at Adrian's throat and caught on something. When his hand came away he was holding the knife and Adrian's tie. I sagged inwardly with sick relief.

He showed it to Wallace. "That's a fancy one, ain't it? These hot-shit rich guys like the good stuff, don't they?"

I shifted a little more to the right to get a better angle on Francis. It would be steep and fast and I'd have to judge it just right when to—

"And lookit these fancy buttons. . . . But maybe they ain't good enough for such a nice shirt. Maybe they oughta be solid gold instead." He dropped the scrap of tie and neatly sliced away a collar button. "Come on, hot shit, I'm talking to you—wake up and lissen."

The point of the knife jabbed Adrian lightly in the side and he jerked, swinging a little from the rope.

"Yeah, hot shit, have a good look at things. You 'member trying to fight me? This is how I pay you back, you see? You *see*?" He laughed at whatever he saw on Adrian's face.

Adrian mumbled something I couldn't catch. Francis looked at Wallace.

"He wants to know if you killed some broad, Dimmy. You kill anyone today?"

"Not that I can remember," said Wallace, his voice flat.

"How come you don't ask *me*, hot shit? Maybe I did it, maybe I walked in and did her good. Maybe she let me in and wasn't friendly enough. That's the sister, huh? Robley's sister? He keeps quiet about her, but we know all about her, and we know all about how to make a girl real friendly. Hey, Dimmy, he's telling me to shut up. What do you think of that?"

Dimmy was bored again and expressed no opinion.

Playing, Francis jabbed the knife at Adrian's face. "That's what I think of shutting up, Mr. Fancy Hot Shit."

I moved a little lower. It would have to be from below. The rack of tires ran all along the wall's length and there was no room to go above them.

"You know you're bleeding? Maybe I should just open it up a little more . . ."

He was very close to Adrian, it was going to be tight.

". . . slip it right between the ribs. I can do it fast or slow—how thick is your skin, Mr. Hot Shit?"

I was nearly too solid. Gravity tugged at me as I pressed my feet against the wall and launched across the open space of the garage like a swimmer into water. I felt the resistance of the air slow me down and countered it by growing more solid. Solidity gave me weight and speed, and when I slammed into Francis with a full body tackle I'd completely materialized.

We crashed into the stacked oil drums, bringing them down

with a stunning amount of sound. One of them fell right on me, cracking my head, and I couldn't move for a moment. With some disgust, I belatedly realized I could have vanished right after hitting Francis and saved myself the discomfort.

A hand plowed in and grabbed the collar of my coat, hauling me out of the mess. I sprawled backward, throwing my arms out for balance, but my rescuer dodged out of range, not that I was in shape to do him harm. My head felt like a small firecracker had gone off just under the spot where the barrel had landed. The metal wasn't as bad as wood, but the pure kinetic shock of all that weight required some recovery time.

Pops appeared from the office, gawking at the chaos and then at me. "Thas one of 'em—the hitcher with that feller who wouldn't leave."

"What?" demanded Wallace.

"I seen 'im walk. How'd he get in here?"

Dimmy Wallace had more cause to wonder about that himself, having witnessed my miraculous appearance out of nowhere. I rubbed the sore spot on my skull and got reoriented. Francis was facedown in the middle of the overturned drums, not moving. I hadn't killed him, but he wouldn't be functioning for some time to come. In front of me was Pops and on my left and coming around to the front was Wallace.

He had a stubby black revolver in his hand. From the tiny size of the barrel opening it looked to be only a twenty-two. They could do damage and could certainly kill, but you had to know how to use them. Since I didn't know what kind of shot he was, I'd have to assume he was an expert and handle things from that angle. Adrian was my prime worry; we were both on the wrong end of the gun, but he'd be the one to get hurt if I weren't careful.

He swung a little against the confines of the barrel. Francis had been so close to him when I came hurtling down that he'd been bumped by the rush. His face was guarded as always, but flushed with a new alertness at my arrival. His eyes were sharp, dark pinpoints, full of sudden questions and something I interpreted as fear.

"You okay?" I asked.

His eyes widened slightly and his mouth twisted open—into

an awful gasping laugh. He shut it down almost as soon as it was out.

"You!" This from Wallace. After that he couldn't seem to think of anything else to say. He'd seen me literally come out of thin air and was having a lot of trouble handling the event. His eyes kept bouncing from me to the rest of the garage, searching for some hiding place that I might have sprung from.

"Looks like Francis is a little flat," I said conversationally. "You want I should pick him up?"

The words didn't really register, which was too bad, as I wanted to distract him from his uncertainty and speculations.

"He was with that car?" he asked Pops.

"I tol' ya," came the confirmation.

Wallace shifted from me to Adrian and back again. "The other guy'll bring help, you can bet on that."

"Then I'm gittin' gone."

"Yeah, go start the truck."

Damn. I'd been hoping to stall him a little longer. I was ten feet away from the gun. Wallace had judged that to be a safe distance to keep me from trying anything. It couldn't be helped, I wasn't about to let them take a free walk out.

I moved a step to the right, widening the space between myself and Adrian. The gun muzzle swung and centered on my chest. Pops froze, his mouth slack, and the bottom gums showing as he waited to see what happened.

"Stay *put*," said Wallace.

His eyes were still blank and I didn't like what wasn't in them. Off to the left Adrian expelled another short hiss of air. I couldn't tell if it was laughter, pain, or fear.

Then Wallace moved one finger. He was fast, there was no way I could have stopped him in time.

The bullet lanced my chest like a white-hot needle, its impact and effect all out of proportion to its size. His aim was perfect, precise as a top surgeon's. It went in just left of my breastbone, slipped between the ribs to clip my heart, and tore out my back.

Time slowed and movement along with it. As a sound separate from the shot, I heard the flat *tink* of lead on steel as it struck one of the barrels behind me. Before the finger could

tighten on the trigger again I was on him. His lips peeled back
as I wrenched the gun away, a mirror of my own pain. The
bullet's tearing flight through my body had nearly knocked me
down from the fire-red shock. I wanted him to feel the same
hurt, I wanted him to know about death. . . .

A short, curse-choked scream.

Adrian's voice shouting my name.

White darkness clouding my sight.

Din-filled silence jamming my ears.

Sound flooded back into my consciousness as though I'd never
heard it before. Time had slowed and then vanished altogether
from my mind. It returned, trickling unevenly as I woke out of
the cold rage that had taken me down to . . . to . . .

I shied away from what lay within me. My body trembled.
The first time this had happened, it hadn't been so bad.
Understanding had come with experience, but that didn't make
it any better. If I'd still been a normal human, I'd have
staggered to the grease pit and been sick.

Dimmy Wallace was on his side at my feet, curled fetuslike
around his broken arm. Pops was gone and distantly I heard the
rough thrum of the truck outside starting up. He'd be well away
by the time I ran out front. The cops could worry about him,
I had troubles of my own.

I turned Wallace over gently, as though to make up for what
I'd done. He mewed out, crying over his ruined arm. His
colorless eyes opened, squinting as though simple sight caused
him pain as well.

Then he bared his teeth and started calling me every foul
name in his ample street vocabulary.

The world shifted abruptly back to normal, and his cursing
washed over my fear and dissipated it. He called me more
names, thinking my laughter was at his agony, then the eyes
widened a little more as he decided I was crazy. I had been, for
one brief, awful moment. Now I was deliriously thankful I'd
not passed the insanity on to him.

"You're staying right where you are, understand?" I made
certain he would obey but didn't bother putting him to sleep. I
had, after all, wanted him to feel pain.

Francis was well and truly out, but I collected his dropped knife and put it in my coat pocket. It clattered against Wallace's gun. Another small tremor fluttered against the base of my spine because I couldn't remember picking the thing up.

I finally stepped clear of Francis and went to Adrian, pulling the knife out again. We locked eyes as I reached above him and cut at the rope. He said nothing, but his gaze dropped after a moment to the hole in my shirt. He'd been awake. He'd seen and heard it happen.

"Bulletproof vest," I said.

"Yes . . . of course," he murmured.

The last strand broke away and he collapsed forward, biting off the agony of release. We had a clumsy moment as I alternately pulled and lifted him from the oil drum. When he was out flat on the filthy floor, he groaned gratefully at the change of position.

"Your hands?" I asked. The skin was swollen and red where the rope had cut into his wrists, but his fingers were still moving a little.

"Can't feel a thing yet. It's my shoulders and back—" He broke off and the creases around his eyes and mouth deepened as he dealt with the inner protests of his body.

Outside, a car rolled up, nearly silent. I only just caught its tires crunching over the road surface. The driver must have cut the motor and coasted in. I told Adrian to keep quiet and cracked open the office door for a look as Wallace had done before me.

I saw a narrow piece of the station and some of the street beyond. Parked across the street, opposite the pumps, was Escott's big Nash. In the distance and coming closer I heard the first siren rise and soar into the pale night sky. I sighed relief and went out to meet them.

Lieutenant Blair had been up all night as well, but suffered the effects more. I was tired, too, but in a different way from him.

"And you say that when you drove off in the car, Charles just slipped into the garage and surprised them?"

"Yeah. I wanted to go in, but he was in charge and said it was his place to do it himself. Somebody had to drive the car away as a distraction and to keep an eye on Miss Steler, so I got the job."

The uniformed cop who took down my original statement had listened to it twice over now with mild interest. His current entertainment came from watching Blair trying to swallow it all. He sat at our table in the hospital canteen, his notebook and pencil on standby in case I decided to change anything. Blair was across from me and fastidiously ignoring the stale cup of coffee someone had brought him.

The canteen was empty except for a woman behind the counter minding the coffee machine and a pile of donuts. She looked more interested in the donuts than us. It was a big hospital for a big city; maybe she was used to cops interviewing people at ungodly hours of the morning.

"Dimmy claims that he shot you," he said.

"Uh-huh." I sounded doubtful. Who was he going to believe, some crook or me? On the other hand, this could prove to be quite a strain on our induced friendship. "If he wants to put a nail in his coffin, that's his business, but it was Charles he shot."

"Really?" It was Blair's turn to sound doubtful and he leaned forward, lacing his fingers together. "And just how did *he* survive?"

"He's got a bulletproof vest. He said Wallace looked pretty rattled when he didn't fall down, maybe that's why there's a mix-up about who got shot."

Blair had done a quick inspection of my clothes and found no trace of a bullet hole. Earlier, Escott and I had hastily switched shirts in the men's room while everyone had been busy with Adrian and the others in emergency. I carried my punctured coat over my arm.

"So Dimmy shot him and it sort of slipped his mind?"

"He's not the type to get worked up about a thing like that."

The cop at the end made a noise and Blair glared at him, then came back to me. "Well, yes, I can see how that could happen, he must get shot several times a week. I'm sure he's used to it by now."

I shrugged good-naturedly. "You'll have to talk to him about it, I missed all the fun."

"I'll bet." He couldn't quite resist putting in some sarcasm, but he was at a dead end and knew it. A change of subject was next. "All right. Now, as to how you knew to go there . . ."

"The gas station? That was Charles's idea."

"Was it?"

"Yeah. He thought maybe Adrian might have gone after Dimmy Wallace because of Sandra—which is how it turned out—and he's got a few connections around town. . . ." Some truths, some falsehoods, they were mixed up enough for me to get away with them.

"What connections?"

I shrugged. "You'll have to ask him."

"I will. How did that reporter get involved?"

"She followed us and wouldn't leave, you know what they're like."

"I know what that one's like," he muttered, and the cop made a noise again and got another glare.

A third cop came in and said that Francis Koller was awake. Blair told me to get lost and went to yet another interview. My old suggestion of friendship was definitely wearing thin.

When they all walked out and left me alone I put my head on my folded arms and felt old in heart, cold in spirit, and tired to the bone. It was a mental weariness, harder to deal with than the physical kind. You can go to bed and rest the body, but the burden of your own emotions can take years to lift, if ever.

"Would you care to go home?" Escott stood in the doorway, hands in his pockets, head cocked to one side.

"Like a week ago. What's the time?"

"A little after five."

Dawn was still too far away. I wanted oblivion now.

"Headache?"

"Yeah, but all over, if you know what I mean."

"Indeed I do. How did things go with Lieutenant Blair?"

"Pretty much as you expected."

"I'm pleased to hear that."

"Said he'd talk to you later."

Escott gave in to an extended and luxuriant yawn. "You take the car, then. I'll find a cab after he's finished his questions with me. Come on, I'll walk you out."

My chair squawked loudly against the floor as it scraped back.

"Will the suggestions you gave to Miss Steler about who did what hold?" he asked.

"I don't think there'll be any problem."

"Let us hope so. With your condition you could hardly put in a court appearance if and when this mess comes to trial."

"Maybe if it were a night court . . . ?"

He smiled. "What about Koller and Wallace?"

"I was able to talk to Wallace before they put him in the ambulance. He didn't kill Sandra but he couldn't say yes or no for Koller. The white coats chased me out before I could tell him what kind of story to give."

"What about Koller?"

"Him I'll have to talk to later, or maybe the cops can sweat it out of him today. I don't think he can back up Wallace's story. I came in so fast he never knew what hit him."

We'd only gone a few yards down the hall when a large nurse stepped from her station and blocked the way. "Mr. Fleming?" She glanced back and forth between us.

"Me," I said, halfheartedly raising a hand.

"One of my patients asked to see you before you left."

"Isn't it past visiting hours?"

"It certainly is," she said wearily. "But he was very insistent."

"Alex Adrian?" I'd been expecting this and dreading it.

"Right this way." She led off without waiting to see if we followed.

Escott politely waited outside as I went into Adrian's private room. He was sitting stiffly against a bank of pillows on the high bed, wearing a flimsy hospital gown and a disgusted expression. Two big wads of bandages covered his wrists and I couldn't help but think of Popeye the Sailor.

"Something amusing you?" he said.

"Just glad you're all right."

"That's one man's opinion."

"The nurse said—"

"Yes, please come in."

His face was drained and gray against the white pillows, and the cloudiness in his dark eyes suggested drugs. In deference to his wrenched shoulders and arms, he was careful not to move his head too much. I took a metal chair next to the bed and turned it around to face him.

"Cops talk to you?" I asked.

"Oh yes. Quite thoroughly and at great length, then that lieutenant told me I'd been damned lucky and to leave police work to the police from now on."

"Nothing like adding insult to injury."

"The insult is that they're not telling me anything. What's to happen to Wallace?"

"I don't know. Last I saw, they'd knocked him out to work on his arm."

"Is anyone watching him or Koller?"

"Yes." I didn't like this turn of the conversation. "Stay away from them, Alex."

He said nothing. A sullen red fire glowed far back in his half-lidded eyes.

"They're in custody and that's enough for now. You can press charges—"

"I already have, for assault and attempted murder, but it is not nearly enough."

"It'll have to be."

He looked straight ahead to the blank white wall in front of him. "If it had been Miss Smythe, what would you do?"

That one hit me hard, as he'd meant it to. Once my gut reaction eased, I realized it had taken a lot out of him to say that, to admit Sandra had made him so vulnerable.

"Same as you, want to tear them to pieces."

His eyes shut, his voice dropped to a gentle whisper. "That's exactly what I want to do to them, and I want to do it with my own hands."

I couldn't hold that against him. I knew exactly how he felt. More so, because in the past I had acted on those feelings and killed.

"Thank you for coming after me," he said in the same quiet tone. The darkness within and around me lessened a little.

"You're welcome."

His breathing evened out and deepened. Whatever they'd

given him was getting a chance to work now. "Did it hurt very much?" he asked.

"Did what?"

"When he shot you."

Hell.

"I once saw a magician shoot at a deck of cards and hit only the ace of spades. . . . Perhaps Wallace had a magical bullet that only puts holes in clothing and not in people."

"What do you want?"

The question surprised him enough to open his eyes. "Nothing, really—only confirmation of what I know I saw. You came diving out of thin air from an impossible angle, then took a smash in the skull that should have knocked you cold for hours—or even killed you."

"Maybe you were a little feverish from hanging there for so long."

"Yes. Perhaps I was, but I'm not now." He looked away from me, a faint glitter coming from beneath his lashes. "I saw you fade and flicker back, like a light bulb losing and then regaining its power. I saw you. I did not imagine it."

Hell and damnation.

"The barrel came crashing down and you dropped under it, and then it rolled away because you weren't there anymore. Wallace only saw you coming out of nowhere, he missed the rest. The other barrels were in the way for him. By the time he'd waded through, you were back again, and solid."

I bit my tongue and waited him out.

"And you got up seconds later, asking *me* if *I* was all right." He laughed faintly, like a ghost. "I might have blacked out then, I might have imagined it all, but not the shot. I was quite wide awake. I saw you take it point blank, I saw the exit hole in your back." His look dared me to contradict him.

I didn't and confirmed things by turning away.

"I thought you were rushing him on momentum alone, that you'd fall at any time, but you didn't. You got to him and he screamed."

"I was breaking his arm."

"It was more than pain; it was like what you did to Koller the other night when you frightened him."

"Maybe I've just got a way with me."

"Yes, you do. I wanted to see your face then, I wanted to see *why* he screamed."

His voice was still low and gentle, but somehow filled the sterile room with vibrations of his . . . hate? That wasn't the right word, it wasn't large enough to encompass the emotions quietly seething from him. I knew and had felt all that he was going through: the rage, the need to do something about it, and the ultimate helplessness when that need is denied. It was different for me; I could free myself, but only at the cost of someone else's sanity. Adrian did not have that terrible luxury. He could only talk, which was why I was so ready to listen.

"I didn't tell the police any of this, of course," he said. "And I can understand why you asked me to lie to the police about you and your friend."

"They'd just think you were crazy, coming at them with a story like that."

"They certainly would."

It would only take a moment and he was more than half-under now. A moment of shifting his thoughts around, a few suggestions, and I'd be safe.

"I won't tell anyone."

He didn't have all of it, just enough to question, to be dangerous.

"You moved very fast, you know—when you went after him. You seemed to flow and merge with the air." He was starting to drift already.

Only a moment to convince him of a false memory, to tell him what he should think. I hesitated, because this acceptance was suddenly very important to me.

"It's quite . . . beautiful." The creases on his skin smoothed as the muscles beneath relaxed.

A touch, a freezing of our eyes and a simple command . . .

". . . beautiful . . ." The glitter submerged under his lids.

I went out quietly so as not to wake him.

"What did he want?" asked Escott, falling into step with me.

"To say thanks."

10

A LONG DAY'S rest restored my tired body, if not my peace of mind. When the sun went down and darkness released me for another night, all the same problems were there, only they'd had time to ripen.

Alex Adrian's name was on the front page of the lesser papers again and even the major ones had placed the story above the fold. They carried virtually identical accounts of Sandra's murder. Later editions mentioned that two suspects were in custody, but Barb Steler had scooped them all with her report on how they'd been captured.

"I find it odd that she does not give your name," said Escott. He was stretched full length on his sofa in the parlor, the papers neatly stacked over his legs and a stiff brandy within easy reach on a table. "Or perhaps it's not so terribly odd, after all."

I'd just come up from the basement when he started talking as though continuing an interrupted conversation. His brain was always working and sometimes he expected people to keep up with him. By now I was used to it, but it usually threw others off balance.

"We had a little talk at the hospital when I was giving back her gun," I said.

"She did a credible job of minimizing your role in the incident. No bright lights and fame for you?"

That one didn't even deserve an answer. The radio was tuned to Escott's usual station, giving us an earful of violins playing

Mozart. With the volume down low, the higher-pitched notes were almost bearable.

He folded the last paper, adding it to the stack on his knees, then inhaled a few molecules of brandy. "I appreciated her free advertisement of my business, but am rather annoyed at being called a 'private detective.'"

It just meant he'd be getting more requests to do divorce cases. He could handle turning them down.

"Learn anything new today?" I asked, sitting across the table from him.

"I was able to glance at the autopsy report."

That had to have taken some doing. Blair hadn't exactly been in a sweet mood when we'd last seen him.

"Sandra Robley had some bruising on her face and the left side of her skull was smashed in by a very powerful blow. The forensic man was of the opinion that she'd first been struck by a fist and then hit with something much harder while she was down. The police found a heavy bronze sculpture by the sink in the Robleys' kitchen. They think the killer took it there to wash away the blood and fingerprints. It was next to a damp towel and quite clean."

"Very neat of the bastard."

"Except for her change purse, nothing else seems to have been stolen."

"You think it was a blind?"

"Yes. Probably the best the killer could do at the time. They had no valuables in the place unless you count their paintings. Except for confidence tricksters or forgers, who are rarely so violent, very few criminals are interested in the fine arts as a source of money."

"What do the cops think?"

"They are of a similar opinion, that it was a blind, but murder for the gain of a few dollars is certainly within their experience. Today they've been questioning Sandra's friends and business acquaintances on the theory that the crime was committed for a personal reason rather than gain. A personal motive is often easily found out—proving one in court is the tricky bit."

"What about Evan?"

"He's recovered enough to give the police a coherent statement, but is still in hospital and under mild sedation."

"He's all right, then?"

"As well as he can be, considering his circumstances."

"What'd he say?"

"That he walked his lady friend home, returned to his own house about an hour later, and discovered his sister's body. He remembers calling Alex Adrian, but has no memory of anything afterwards. His doctor says the amnesia is not unexpected, he may recover or he may not."

"Do the police believe him?"

"They confirmed the times of arrival and departure with the lady, which was also corroborated by her roommate. Both vouched for his good character in the most sincere terms and also stated that Evan was in a lighthearted, very humorous mood. Of course, the man could be a consummate actor or a liar who so believes in his own fantasies that he is able to convince others."

"He doesn't strike me as the type, if there's a type for him to be."

"I'm merely covering all possibilities. As for practicalities, he had the means and opportunity, but no readily apparent motive. I'm not saying the police have entirely ruled him out as a suspect, but thus far they have yet to arrest him."

"That's something at least. How's your new client doing?"

"Mr. Brett came to the office long enough to drop off his contract and to listen to an expurgated version of how we found Adrian. He then signed a check and left for the hospital to see Evan."

"He paid you already?"

"For one day's—or rather night's—work. He's satisfied that Wallace and Koller are responsible for Sandra's death."

"Are you?"

His eyes were firmly fixed on his brandy snifter. "They do seem to be tailor made for the part, and their violent response to Adrian's intrusion was most incriminating. Since Wallace is not powerful enough to challenge Gordy directly, their motive for murder could be a form of reprisal against Evan Robley."

"Shaky, Charles."

"I know. From what you've told me, they would have been more likely to want to frighten the Robleys and thus intimidate Evan into continuing payment on his canceled debt. Murdering his prime source of income is certainly carrying things too far. Wallace and Koller are denying all knowledge of it."

"They'd have to. Any news on the old geezer from the garage?"

"The police located him later that morning, he's assisting in their inquiries—oh yes, they also found the other fellow, Toumey."

"Yeah?"

"He'd taken Adrian's coupe around to a certain garage to sell to the less-than-honest operators there. They have, or rather had, a highly lucrative stolen-car business. The police alert to pick up Adrian included a description of his vehicle and its license number, and a passing patrol car happened to be in the right place at the right time. Several birds were annihilated with the casting of that particular stone."

"So Adrian's off the hook with the cops?"

"Yes, for the time being."

"You think he did it?"

"I think we lack information." He'd stare a hole in that brandy snifter if he wasn't careful.

"And you figure I should talk to him?"

He nodded once, but remained silent, letting me think. Damn the son of a bitch. The Mozart stuff ended and was replaced by some kind of modern vocal piece that sounded like stuttering, lovesick cats. I heaved to my feet.

"I'll see you later."

I didn't take a direct route but dropped by Bobbi's hotel to check on her. I'd tried calling from Escott's, but her phone was busy.

Piano music came through the walls, which meant Marza was visiting. I grimaced, but then no one ever said life was fair, and knocked on the door. The music faltered over a few notes and then continued on with determination. She usually kept the mute pedal down for the sake of the other hotel tenants, but shifted her foot from it as Bobbi let me in.

We hugged hello and Bobbi asked her to stop playing so we could talk.

Marza put on a sweet smile, utterly lacking in sincerity. "I'm sorry, was I disturbing anyone?" She pretended to busy herself by lighting one of her noisome little cigars. To protect my own sanity, I grabbed Bobbi and dragged her out into the hall and firmly shut the door behind us.

"Rude, isn't she?" I asked.

"Absolutely," she answered, and then we gave each other a proper kiss.

"Your phone's been busy," I said when she came up for air.

"It started ringing when the papers came out this morning. I'm just famous enough locally to bring every crank out of the woodwork, so I had to take it off the hook. Did you see one of those rags? 'Singer Stumbles Over Slaying.' I just hope they don't cancel my spot this Saturday." She pulled me tight, needing reassurance. "This is awful, thinking about myself with all this going on."

"No, it's not. You couldn't be awful if you tried, unlike some people I know." I nodded significantly at the door and Marza's direction and eventually got a smile.

"I'm sorry about that, she thinks you've dragged me into a situation that will hurt me. Marza's terribly protective."

"She's terribly something. Are you doing all right?"

"Yes, I'm just fine, really. Did you have anything to do with finding Alex?"

I gave her the quick version of events and covered the points all the papers missed. "Anyway, the heat's off him for now."

"What about poor Evan? I've tried calling the hospital, but they just said he was stable, whatever that means."

"Charles says he's all right, he just doesn't remember much from last night."

"Probably just as well. Look, I'm going to kick Marza out so we don't have to hang around the hall."

"Sorry, baby, but I have to go talk with Alex about some things."

"Like whether he—"

"Yeah, that and some other stuff."

"I don't know whether to wish you luck or not. Can you come back by later?"

"As soon as I'm free."

"Good. I'm still going to kick Marza out. She's been with me almost all day and I need a break."

"Atta girl."

At the hospital, the nurse on Evan's floor told me only thirty minutes were left for visiting.

"Is he still under medication?"

"Yes, a mild sedative to relax him."

That was convenient. "Has he had any other visitors?"

"Some of his friends are with him now." Her phone rang before I could ask which ones.

I opened his door quietly and was not too surprised to see Reva Stokes and Leighton Brett. Reva was concentrating on her talk with Evan and didn't notice me, but Brett looked up in time. He was a big man, but still managed to ease out soundlessly, heaving a relieved sigh as he joined me in the hall. He smiled grimly and pumped my hand.

"Good of you to come by like this," he said. "I hope you don't mind waiting, but Reva's just gotten him to talk a little about Sandra, and an interruption now might spoil the mood."

"I understand. How's he doing?"

"Better than he was last night. I forgot to thank you for your help. When he started to go off the deep end—"

"We were just lucky that doctor was still hanging around. Is Evan's memory any better?"

" 'Fraid not. I'm hoping Reva can help him, but if it comes to it I'll be looking around for some kind of psychiatrist. I don't know about you, but that breakdown he had last night scared me to death, and I'm still worried about him."

"How so?"

"He might do something crazy if we don't watch him. He and Sandra were very close. They genuinely liked each other. Now, I like my own sister, but if she got killed—God forbid—I wouldn't do anything desperate to myself out of grief. Anyway, that's how Evan's worrying me."

"Does his doctor know about this?"

"I've talked to him. He's keeping Evan sedated for the most part, but whether that's doing him any good . . ." Brett finished with a shrug.

"How long will he be here?"

"He gets out tomorrow and then he's coming to our house. I'm not letting him go back to that apartment and stay there alone."

"I'm glad to hear that, but I thought since he's known Alex for so long . . ."

He snorted, but not unkindly. "Alex is hardly fit to take care of himself, much less Evan."

"He's survived."

"At the cost of his soul, if you ask me. He gave up when his wife died. All we're seeing now is the walking corpse."

Brett had a point there. The first time I met Adrian I thought the same myself. "He seemed pretty lively last night."

"Oh, he still has some anger in him. That's what sent him off half-cocked and nearly got him killed. I think anger is all that's really keeping him going these days, which is not a good way to live. I'd like to get *him* to a psychiatrist, but you can't cure a man's mind unless he wants help in the first place."

"I can understand him being angry about Sandra, but—"

"About his wife? It's been there, all mixed up with his grief. The man can twist himself up so much he could meet himself coming around a corner. Alex was working in his studio the night Celia—the night she died."

"And if he hadn't been painting, he might have stopped her?"

Brett nodded. "He's angry with himself and sometimes it's thick enough to cut with a knife. Evan was able to put up with it because he's known him for so long and is so easygoing he can't stay mad at anyone for more than a minute."

"Has Alex been in to see him?"

"I don't know. He was released earlier today and isn't answering his phone."

That sounded familiar. Brett excused himself to look in on Reva and a few minutes later they both emerged.

"I'm glad you've come by," she told me, taking my hand briefly. "He's still very sleepy."

"I won't stay long," I promised, and wished them a good night. When they were well down the hall, I went into Evan's room.

He was motionless on the high metal bed, his lank, ash-colored hair clinging damply to his pasty gray forehead. One lamp burned in a corner, its shade tilted so the light wouldn't bother him. He didn't notice I was in the room until I sat down next to him and lightly touched his hand.

He started slightly and his eyes dragged open. "Wha . . . ?"

"Hi, remember me?"

Recognition tugged wanly at the corners of his mouth. "Where's that pretty lady of yours?"

"I had to leave her home, I've heard of your reputation."

"You and all the nurses on this floor. Any water around?"

I found a glass on the bedside table and filled it for him. He sat up for a sip and fell back, exhausted. "They pumped me full of something I don't like. Everything tastes awful, even the water."

"How do you feel?"

"Dunno . . . wrapped up in cotton, all over. When I'm out of here I'll find something else to do the job."

Brett's fears were still fresh in my mind, but I had the feeling Evan was referring to the kind of emotional painkiller you get from a bottle of booze. "Cops give you a hard time?"

His eyes went vague for a second. "I don't think so, it's all so fuzzy."

"I know."

"This is real, isn't it? She's gone, isn't she?"

I nodded.

His hands formed into helpless fists and went slack again. "Why?"

"I don't know, Evan. I'm very sorry."

Not unexpectedly, tears started out of his eyes and trailed down the sides of his face. He was unaware of them.

I'd seen him start up like this before and neither of us would be the better for a repeat performance. "Evan . . . listen to me . . ."

First I calmed him down and then we had a quiet talk. It didn't take long to reach through to his blocked memory and find out he'd told the complete truth to the police. At least I had my own private confirmation that he hadn't killed Sandra and knew nothing about it. The last thing I did before sending him off to sleep was to make sure he had no thoughts about suicide.

I stood and turned to leave—and stopped short. Adrian was standing just inside the door. His mouth was slightly open and he was twisting his wedding band around. I'd been focused entirely on Evan and had heard nothing.

"Hello," I said, hoping it didn't sound as awkward as I felt.

"I was wondering if you might show up," he stated neutrally. He was casually dressed, his shirtsleeves rolled back to accommodate all the bandaging on his wrists.

"How are you?" I asked.

"Well enough."

"Been there long?"

"Oh, yes."

"I'd like to talk to you."

"I rather thought you might. Shall we find a more comfortable place to do so?"

Not waiting for a reply, he led the way down the corridor to a spacious room with one wall composed mostly of windows. Chairs and tables dotted the polished floor at frequent intervals, and a row of wheelchairs were stored in a far corner. During the day the place would have been flooded with sunlight, but now it was gloomy and strangely isolated. He didn't bother turning on the high overhead lamps and was content to remain in what for him would be darkness.

"It's like your studio, isn't it?" I asked.

He arrested his move to pull a chair from a table and glanced around. "Yes, it is . . . I'd wondered why I liked this place."

"And you prefer sitting in the dark?"

He got the chair the rest of the way out and sank gratefully into it. His movements were slow and careful, an indication of the stiffness lingering in his shoulders and back. "I don't mind. It softens reality and makes the impossible more acceptable."

"Me, for instance?"

"Yes." He brought out a pack of cigarettes and tapped one onto the table, but didn't fire up his match. Perhaps even that tiny spark would have made things too real for him. "I meant what I said last night, I won't tell anyone about you—or about what I just saw."

"Thanks."

"I have a lot of questions, though," he added.

"I might not answer them."

"You've a right to your privacy." He played with the cigarette, turning it end over end between his index finger and thumb. "Were you born with your abilities or were they acquired?"

"Acquired."

"Are there others like you?"

"I know of only two others."

"What are you?"

I considered that one seriously for a few seconds, then started to laugh. I couldn't help myself. Adrian looked vaguely insulted at first, then broke into one of his sudden smiles. It was brief, on and off again, but he meant it.

"Sorry," I said.

He shrugged it away and finally lit his cigarette, blowing smoke up into the still air. "Yes, I can see I'm ridiculous."

"Not you, the situation. Wanna change the subject?"

"By all means."

I broke away from the door and took one of the other chairs at his table. "Sandra."

Muscles on both sides of his neck tightened into iron. "No."

"Have to."

"Why? No . . . never mind, it's all too obvious. As with Evan, you want to know if I murdered her."

"You need to be eliminated from a list of possibles."

"Same thing, nicer phrasing." He looked directly at me, his eyes and voice like ice. "Ask."

I did and got the answer I expected. While I had his attention I asked my other question. "Did you kill Celia?"

His reply was slow in coming, so slow in fact that he woke out of my influence in his fight to hold it in. His walls were back up again but not as solid as before. When he took a puff from his cigarette I noticed the slight tremor in his hand. "I did not kill my wife," he whispered. "Not directly."

"How, then, indirectly?"

He was quiet for so long I thought I'd have to give him another nudge. "My work," he said finally, his tone so faint I might have imagined the words. "Always my damned work."

I waited until he'd smoked another half inch. "Your work?"

"What I have is not artistic talent, it's addiction. It's always been there, all my life. The silence and total solitude are utterly necessary for me to produce. Not many people can understand that, least of all Celia. She did try, and God knows she loved me, but it must have been the bitterest thing of all for her to realize she would always be second to the art."

I knew how bitter it had been for Barb Steler.

"I believe that all people have the need to create, and consciously or not they find outlets for it. They paint or write, they marry and have children. Celia had no such outlets for herself, but the need was there, so eventually she found one."

"What do you mean?"

"Another man. I really don't know how long it went on. She had the most miserable excuses for being out and sometimes she couldn't keep her stories straight. Even now I'm not sure if I was being selectively blind or just stupid, probably a bit of both. She wanted me to find out, like a child who does something bad for the sake of getting attention."

"Did you?"

"Yes. Sooner or later every sleeper wakes. I think she was glad when it happened. It was quite an explosion on my part, but it proved to her I could still be hurt—that I still loved her." Some of his inner agony welled up, constricting his throat, thickening his voice. "Two days later she went out to the garage and started the car."

He drew deeply on the cigarette to distract himself and coughed a little on the smoke. If there was a suppressed sob hidden in that cough, I pretended not to notice.

"I was on the other side of the house in the studio and heard nothing. I'd been avoiding her by working on another damned magazine cover. We'd talked divorce, neither of us really wanted it, but we didn't know how to return to each other. I didn't know how to forgive her. She broke it off the only way she felt she could." He stared out the tall windows, seeing nothing. "That's how I killed her."

"Did Sandra know about this?"

"No. I wanted things to be different for us. She would have always been first—I would have made certain of it. We never had the chance."

"Who was the man?"

"Celia never told me."

"Could it have been Evan?"

He was almost amused. "No, of course not. He talks a lot of charm to a lot of women, but has the sense to stay away from the married ones. Besides, at that time he was happily involved with a little blond model named Carol."

"Have you ever figured out who it was, or guessed?"

He shook his head and stubbed out the cigarette in a tin ashtray. "I used to think of nothing else and now it hardly seems to matter anymore."

"You've no idea?"

"None." He ticked at the ashtray with an idle finger and nearly sent the dregs flying. "I think I'll look in on Evan now."

"He's going home with Reva and Leighton tomorrow."

"I thought they might make the offer, if only to spare him from my cheerful company. They did the same for me when Celia died, but I knew I'd smother beneath all their concern for my well-being. Evan's the type to respond to such care, though. Perhaps it's what's best for him."

"I hope so."

"Good night." He walked out slowly, hardly making a sound.

". . . so if Charles is still up when I go home he'll be getting an earful."

Bobbi half reclined on her couch, her feet curled under her and a small coffee in her hand. I sat opposite her on the edge of a low table, rubbing my right fist into my left palm.

"You think Celia and Sandra are connected?" she asked.

"They were both involved with Alex Adrian."

"He really got to you, huh?"

"Because of losing Maureen, I see myself in him. I know how he feels."

"You want to help, but you can't."

"In a nutshell," I said, sighing. "Your phone back on the hook?"

"Not yet, you need to use it?"

"No, I'm just noticing the quiet a lot for some reason."

"Stop carrying the world on your back and things will get a lot noisier for you."

She raised a smile out of me again. "Want to go to a movie?"

"How 'bout a western with a nice cattle stampede?"

That made me blink, until I figured out what she was getting at. "Been thinking about visiting the Stockyards?"

"All day."

"If you're sure . . ."

"Not yet, but you said I should watch what you do."

"I know. I think you have less problems handling it than I do."

"We can find out."

"Okay. Go put on something you don't mind getting dirty. That place ain't exactly Michigan Avenue, you know."

Ten minutes later we were cuddled up in the front seat of my car. Bobbi wore some battered Oxfords, a dark sweater, and a matching pair of wide-legged ladies' trousers. Her bright hair was covered by a black cloche hat she said she hated, but hadn't gotten around to throwing out yet. We didn't talk much, but it was a companionable silence. I drove sedately and parked fairly close in.

The air vibrated with the lowing of hundreds of animals, and their organic stench flooded over us. Normally I wouldn't have parked downwind, but it was convenient. The car would air out when we left. I glanced at Bobbi to see if she was ready to chicken out. She seemed to read my mind and shook her head with a smile.

"How do we get inside?"

"I usually disappear and float in, like I did the other night through Evan's door. This time we'll climb a fence."

She opened her handbag and pulled out a tattered pair of black cotton gloves. "Just as well I came prepared. I don't want to pick up any splinters." She pulled them on and tossed the bag under the car seat. "Ready?"

"You been studying for this?"

"I had a lot of time to think about it."

Picking a long, dark stretch between streetlights, I led the way in and helped her climb up and over. No one was around to notice our intrusion, but I didn't want to take any chances by hanging around too long. We went to the closest occupied pen and scrambled over its thick timbers.

Bobbi stared at the three cows huddled in the far corner and they stared unenthusiastically back. "Big, aren't they?"

"They stink, too."

"But you put your mouth—"

"Baby, I get so hungry, it just doesn't matter." A lazy stream of wind from a distant slaughterhouse carried a breath of the bloodsmell over us. Bobbi couldn't pick it up, but I could and it stirred dark things within me.

"Are you hungry now?"

"I'm getting there." I'd fed last night, but a person can be full of food, walk past a restaurant, and still salivate. The same principle applied now. I made myself breathe regularly to catch more of the smell and centered my attention on the nearest animal.

The process of hypnotizing people is fairly simple, but different rules apply to animals because they have less intellect and better defensive instincts. I didn't entirely understand how to make an animal stand still for me, it was on the same level as my ability to disappear: I'd think about it and it happened, like flexing an invisible muscle. Maybe the animals could sense it somehow; it didn't matter much to me as long as it worked.

I closed in on the cow and ran my hand lightly over a big surface vein. It remained still, as though I weren't there. Bobbi tiptoed closer to see things better.

"This is where I usually go in," I told her, keeping my voice low and even. She nodded her understanding.

"What about your teeth?"

My canines had not yet emerged. I wasn't really all that hungry, nor was I sexually aroused to any great degree. "I'm having a problem there."

"Maybe I could help?" Her intuition was working again. That, or she correctly read the look in my eye.

"If you don't mind a little smooching in a cattle pen . . ." She didn't.

A few minutes later I had to pull away from her. "I should have brought you along sooner, it's a lot more fun like this."

"Just as long as you don't feel the same way about the cow."

"Good grief, no."

The animal hadn't moved. I crouched next to it, careful to keep my knees out of the muck, and centered in on the vein. Not so very long ago I'd been quite squeamish about the whole business, now I cut straight through without any fuss—and I drank.

Bobbi crowded in to see. I finished and wiped my lips and she patted the cow. "Nothing shows, at least nothing I can see now," she said.

"They get worse battering on the trip in."

"Maybe you should keep one as a pet."

"Charles hates cattle, too messy for him. So—what do you think?"

She shrugged. "It's not what I expected."

"And what was that?"

"I'm not sure . . . maybe that you'd sprout horns or something or start foaming at the mouth. Actually, you looked like you were enjoying it."

"Maybe I should start selling tickets."

"Get an agent first. Shall we go?"

"Thought you'd never ask."

We went back to her place and she shucked out of her old clothes while I flushed some soap and hot water over my face. When I came out of the bathroom I immediately noticed the lights were out and that she hadn't bothered to get dressed again.

"Something on your mind?" I asked innocently.

"I'd like to take up where we left off in the cattle pen." She slid her arms around my neck and fastened lightly onto my lips. "That is, unless you think you've already had too much for one night . . ."

She stifled a shriek as I picked her up and carried her to the bed. We fell into it, laughing, and proceeded to do some delightfully indecent things to each other. Between the giggles and gasps, we talked of love and, eventually, consummated it.

Bobbi dozed a little and I stared at the dull white bowl of her overhead lamp, drifting in a pleasant haze of good feeling. Our legs and most of my clothes were tangled up in the sheets, but at the moment it seemed like too much trouble to straighten things out. Elsewhere in the hotel two radios played, each at a different station, but faint enough so as not to be annoying. Outside, traffic sounds oozed in through the windows.

"What are you smiling at?" she murmured.

"You were right. The world isn't so quiet since I put it down and started listening."

"I'm a font of wisdom," she agreed, and stretched luxuriously.

"Have you thought about what comes next?"

"You mean about changing me?"

"Uh-huh."

She snuggled in closer. "Well, it's kind of scary, but then so's love."

"How can love be scary?"

"It just is; the most important things always are."

"You scared of me?"

"Never, but you're still important."

"That's good. What do you want to do?"

She propped up on one elbow and looked at me. "I want to spend forever with you, or at least try."

Damn if I didn't start to get a lump in my throat. I pulled her close and couldn't let her go for the longest time.

"Jack . . . ?"

"Mm?"

"You may not breathe, but I still . . ."

I opened my arms a little and she emerged, smiling, her hair as rumpled as the sheets. "What do we do?" she asked.

I stroked the whole length of her body as though for the first time, making new discoveries, tasting new tastes. They say when you make love to produce a child it's different, more intense and vital. I felt that now and savored it. This was something to always be remembered and I wanted it to be the best of all possible memories for both of us.

She moved against me and on top of me, her warmth soaking into my own flesh. With her I had no need of sunlight. I spread my arms to her and her hands generated new heat where they touched me.

Her lips plucked at my face, my chest, my neck. . . .

That felt wonderful. I encouraged her to continue.

Her blunt human teeth wouldn't be able to break the skin easily, but the touch of them was maddening. I caressed her long, smooth back and worked my hand around front, between us, to her flat stomach. She lifted a little and I moved my hand lower. Her sighs lengthened, matching my own.

The clean scent of her rose perfume filled me, the roar of her heart deafened me, the weight of her body on mine was a delightful burden I never wanted to set down.

She lifted her head, arching it back, her mouth open in a breathless cry as she accepted the climax I gave her. Her legs went stiff, her arms wrapped convulsively around me. Her hair and skin glowed in the faint light from the window. Dear God, she was beautiful.

My other hand came up, because I couldn't stand to wait any longer. With one of my fingernails I dug into my neck over the large vein. I felt no pain, only a sudden trail of scarlet fire seeping onto the flesh.

She saw—and understood. She kissed my lips once and then put her own to the wound. My sigh stretched into a moan as she took from me and as I gladly gave. I'd never had this kind of a climax before, not as a human, not even with Maureen. Like a storm, it rolled over and through and went soaring up to a peak lasting as long as she drew on my red life, taking its promise into herself.

11

"COME *ON*, JACK, this isn't funny."

Something energetically tugged and shook my arm, hard enough to wake the dead.

"Wake *up*."

"Mmm?"

The shaking stopped. "Are you in there? Wake up and answer or I'll get a bucket of water and—"

"Mmm!" I was more affirmative this time and waved her off. " 'M 'wake already." My voice was slurred and it was an uphill battle just to open my eyes.

"So convince me," she insisted.

After a bit of concentration I managed to keep the lids up long enough for a glimpse at her face. Her expression was an interesting combination of anger and worry. "Whas the 'mergency?"

"You are. You haven't moved for hours. I thought I'd killed you."

I considered the heavy feeling of pleasure that still dragged at my edges. "What a great way to go."

"Are you all right? What happened?"

"Just having a little rest. I should have warned you that I might conk out afterwards. Is it very late?"

"A little after ten. You mean that's normal for you when we do it this way?"

"Yeah, but don't worry, it feels just great." I reached for her and pulled her close, craving her softness again. "I think it happens because of my blood loss."

"But you'd just eaten, sort of. I couldn't have taken that much from you."

"I think this had less to do with amount and more to do with sensation."

"Does it hurt you?"

"Anything but. How do you feel?"

"Fine, I guess. You just scared me with that stunt—I mean, you were so *still*."

"Maybe you wore me out."

"Is that how you sleep during the day?"

I nuzzled her hair again. "That's right. Having second thoughts?"

"It's a little late for that, this is just healthy curiosity."

"I'm all in favor of any kind of healthy activity."

"No kidding." She burrowed a little closer and a low laugh bubbled from her. "You know, one of my friends says sometimes it's so good for her she passes out. Is that what happened to you?"

"Yes, my sweet love. That's what happened to me. Accept it as a tribute to your talent and its effect on me."

"Wow."

And that said it all for some time and we held lazily on to each other until she stirred and stated she was starving—for solid food.

"Take you out?" I offered.

She stretched. "Maybe tomorrow; all I want are a couple of scrambled eggs and then I have to sleep. I've got to get up to rehearse at the radio station and then work out what I'm going to wear at this broadcast."

"How come you get dressed to the nines for a radio show? Your audience can't see you."

"The ones in the studio can, and so do all the people I work with. Another thing is that I sing better when I know I look good."

"Oh."

"Besides, the other women dress up and I'm not about to have any of them see me at less than my best."

"You dress for other women?"

"Oh, Jack, it's only showing a little competitiveness."

"And I thought I'd put you out of the running."

"You have, but I don't want people thinking I don't care how I look anymore."

"Bobbi, you'd look like a queen even in a gunnysack."

"I'm glad you think so, but I still wouldn't be caught dead wearing one. Now give me a kiss and let me go fix some food."

A short while later she was slipping some butter yellow scrambled eggs onto a plate along with a slice of dry toast. "If I do change, I think I'm going to miss this stuff a lot. You said you missed the socializing but not the food?"

"That's right." I gulped queasily at the cooking odors and watched in fascinated horror as she dropped a dollop of ketchup on the plate. Even before I'd changed, I'd never liked eggs with ketchup; mustard, maybe, but never ketchup.

"If we do this exchange again, are you going to pass out the same way?"

I must have had a sappy look on my face. It wouldn't be the first time. "I certainly hope so."

"What, do it again or pass out?"

"Well, they both felt terrific. . . ."

She laughed and attacked her eggs while they were still hot, but she sobered again after a few bites. "One more question?"

"As many as you like."

"Was it this way for you with Gaylen, I mean when she . . ." she faltered. "Maybe I shouldn't have asked."

Something in my manner must have stiffened up and she'd noticed right away. "No, it's okay. I still have some scar tissue left, is all, it just isn't where you can see it."

"And with Gaylen?" she prompted, her brow puckered.

I closed my hand gently over hers and told the utter truth. "What you and I did together was make love. What she did to me was a kind of rape. There are a hundred hells of difference between the two."

Escott was still up when I got back home, which I half expected, as he often kept late hours himself. What I did not expect was the presence of a visitor as evidenced by a car standing in my usual spot in front of his house. I recognized it, parked farther down the block, and walked back, wondering if I should just barge in on them or not. Barb Steler had left him with quite a favorable impression of herself; if she in turn found him even a little attractive, my unexpected arrival might not be too welcome. My own ecstatic experience with Bobbi had left me mellow and wishing the same joy upon others, but on the other hand I wanted to know why Barb had come calling.

Curiosity won out and I used my key this time to go inside. If Escott found her irresistible, he was enough of a gentleman to take her upstairs rather than risk a fall from his narrow sofa. In that case I was prepared to become diplomatically deaf and leave the house for an hour or so.

But they were talking about the European situation in his front room and the thought crossed my mind that at times Escott could be an idiot.

". . . Spain is merely the testing ground in a larger game. It's certainly no secret now about Hitler supplying Franco with pilots as well as planes."

"And from this you believe that he has larger ambitions?" she asked, her voice all soft and throaty.

"Larger than any man in history has dared to imagine."

"Today Germany, tomorrow the world?" I could almost see her depreciatory smile. "It is an awfully *large* world."

"Filled with many who would only too cheerfully give up their right to think if they believed it would buy them a little peace and prosperity. It's what he's counting on."

"But think of the good that he's done—"

"Like hiding all the anti-Semitic propaganda for the duration of the Olympic games? Such extreme attitudes directed at a specific population have absolutely no place in an enlightened twentieth-century state, and yet this is the spoken policy of that state's leader. It is hardly a position appropriate for a reasonable and responsible society to take, and yet he has many followers on both sides of the Atlantic."

"Surely you don't intimate that I—"

"Ah, but you equate my general views as a personal attack

on yourself and you needn't. Playing the devil's advocate has its appeal and makes for a better debate. I rather enjoy a good debate."

"And politics are a favorite subject?"

"Not in particular, but one may extrapolate from the larger overview politics provide and distill it down to simple motivations. Hitler's outstanding hatred for Jews most certainly has its root in some personal experience. The man is in sad and desperate need of some sort of mental counseling. He certainly has no business running a country."

"One might say the same for many other world leaders, mightn't one? But then who would be left in charge to run things?"

"The civil service, of course. They may be as slow to change as a bone into a fossil, but are generally more stable than fanatical, slogan-spouting dictators."

She laughed, low and musically, and I made some noise shutting the door. Escott called out from the front room.

"Jack? Come in and join us, my dear fellow, we've been having a most interesting talk on world affairs."

I stuck my hat on the coat tree and sauntered in. Escott was at his ease in his leather chair and Barbara was comfortably ensconced on the couch. Cigarette smoke swirled in the air above the brass lamp by the window and each of them had had at least one mixed drink. For a man of Escott's quiet personal habits, this was practically a New Year's blowout on Times Square.

Barbara patted an empty spot on the couch, smiling fondly at me. "Yes, do come in and help us solve everything."

"Well, uhh . . ."

Escott gave me a very slight high sign, indicating he wanted more company. Not only could he be an idiot, but he wanted a chaperon, too. To each his own, I thought, and dragged my mind away from carnality and myself into the room. I sat on the other end of the couch from Barbara and smiled easily at her. She returned it just as easily and still managed to inject it with a potent shot of her own special electricity. Some people are like that, and her more than most. I wondered why she buried herself working for a cheap tabloid instead of a larger paper.

"You're looking tired, Jack," she observed. "Are you all right?"

"I've been busy."

Escott was very interested, but said nothing because of Barbara's presence.

"Is this a social call?" I asked her.

"I like to think of all my visits as social calls, but not everyone is of the same mind on that."

"Miss Steler came by with some news concerning Dimmy Wallace," Escott prompted.

"What news?"

She shifted forward a little and lost some of her affectations. "He's still being held on other charges, but the police have dropped him as a suspect for Sandra Robley's murder."

I wasn't too surprised at that and said so.

"Then you don't think he did it anyway?"

"No, not really. Why did they drop the charges and what about Koller?"

"Both of them have an alibi for the time."

"What kind of alibi?"

"Wallace's car broke down on the other side of the city and a Father Philip Glover of St. Mary's and two other priests stopped to play good Samaritan. They gave him a lift to a garage and back again, then stayed with him to make sure his car was in working order. He's covered for the whole time of Sandra's murder and then some. Koller stayed behind, but went across the street to wait in a bar. There are several witnesses to confirm that."

"It's too good to be true. Are you sure about these priests?"

"Father Glover is a well-known figure and has served the parish for the last twenty years or so."

"What about the bar?"

"It's one of those little neighborhood taverns where everyone knows everyone else. That's why they noticed Koller; he didn't seem to fit in."

"What were they doing on the other side of town?"

"Minding their own business, they claim. Perhaps they were on a collection trip, but all that really matters is that their alibi is solid and now Alex is back as suspect number one."

"But he nearly got killed himself because he thought Wallace and Koller did it."

"Which doesn't matter to the police. All they know is that he was closely involved with Sandra and can't account for his time that night."

"And that he's under a cloud from another woman's death."

Her look lanced through me with the same kind of force and intent as Wallace's gunshot. Escott had been quiet before, now he turned to stone waiting to see what happened. She drew a deep breath as though to call me a few names, but changed her mind and let it out very slowly.

"I hope you will believe that I am trying to help him now. Or perhaps you're testing me again?" There was enough ice in her voice to start a new glacier, a suitable contrast to the fire in her eyes.

"We all need to be aware of what he's up against, that's why I mentioned it. I know you're trying to help, or you wouldn't be here."

The fires banked, at least for the moment, but she was anything but happy at being reminded of her past smear campaign.

"Are the cops planning to arrest him?" I asked.

"I think so, but word is they're waiting until they've finished talking with all of the Robleys' friends and business contacts. Unless they turn up something from that end . . ." She shrugged.

"He will want a decent lawyer," said Escott.

She turned on him. "And do you think he's guilty?"

He was looking at me. I shook my head. "No, but he is in deep enough trouble to require one all the same. Perhaps you know of someone who might be useful."

"I do, but what else can be done?"

"Little enough at the moment. We and the police require more information than is presently available."

"I suppose a signed confession from the murderer would be nice." She'd put an acid bite to her tone.

"It would be decidedly convenient. Who knows what the future may hold?"

Barbara did not share his optimism one bit. "Nothing more than a jail cell for the rest of Alex's life unless we do something for him." The sarcasm had no effect on Escott, which annoyed her. She got her gloves from her purse and started pulling them on. "Well, gentlemen, it *is* getting late. Jack, would you see me out to my car? The street might not be very safe at this time of night."

I remembered the derringer she carried and figured she wanted talk, not protection, but walked her out anyway.

"How *do* you put up with him?" she asked, turning and leaning back against the closed door of her car.

"It's mutual respect. Besides, he has to put up with me as well."

"That *must* be amusing."

"We're doing what we can about this, Barbara."

She smiled, just a little, and touched my cheek with one finger. "I know, and I'm being terribly ungrateful, especially after the way your friend charged in there to save Alex."

Last night's editing of her memory was still holding, so not everything was going down the drain. "Yeah, he's good at that kind of thing."

"What else has he done?"

"In general or about this case?"

"Both. I'm thinking of writing a feature article on him. 'The Lonely Life of a Detective' or something like that."

"First off, he calls himself a private agent, not a detective, and second, you need to talk to him about what he does."

"You think he might object to his name appearing in my paper?" My hesitation in answering did not insult her. "Don't worry, I have no illusions concerning the kind of rag I work for."

"Why work for them, then?"

"Why not?"

"Because you're too good for them."

"I'm glad you think so. The truth is that I like what I do and will continue to do it until something I like better comes along."

"*Is* there anything you like better?"

Her smile broadened and she traced a finger down the side of my face. "I think you know the answer to that, darling Jack. The problem with my little pleasures is that I don't want to earn my living by them, then they would cease to be so pleasurable."

I didn't know what to say to that and she thoroughly enjoyed my discomfiture.

"You *are* such a sweet man. Would you like to come by later for a drink?"

If she only knew what that invitation really meant to me. "Not tonight—"

"Yes, you do still look tired. What have you been doing?"

"Visiting friends." I started to laugh. "It can be draining."

She picked up on the humor, even if she didn't get the joke. "Another time, then"—she pecked my cheek, got into the car, and slid over to the driver's side—"when you're fully rested." It wasn't what she said, but the way she said it. As she drove off, I stood in the cloud of her exhaust and gulped a few times.

Maybe Escott wasn't such an idiot, after all; it probably had to do with his instinct for self-preservation. I quickly retreated into the house, locking the door for good measure.

He was still in his chair, only now he'd drawn his legs up so his knees bumped his sharp chin, and he'd lit a pipe. He broke off staring into space when I returned and flopped wearily on the sofa.

"A tiring night?" he inquired.

"More than you'll ever know."

"I have observed that when you employ your special talents it often leaves you in a depleted state. May I conclude that you had occasion to use them this evening?"

"Oh, yes."

"Miss Steler prevented you from speaking out, I'm sure, but if you are not too fatigued I should like to hear an account of what happened."

I gave him his earful on my hospital visit, but left out Bobbi and the new phase in our relationship, though he was unabashedly fascinated by my condition and anything to do with it. Hearing about our exchange of blood would no doubt interest him on a certain cold, academic level, but at this point the current state of my emotional life wasn't relevant to the Robley case, nor was it really his business.

By the time I'd wound down, he'd finished his first pipe and was busy reloading another. The air was getting too thick for talk so I got up, opened the front windows, and flushed out my clogged lungs.

"Do you plan to do anything about him?" he asked, successfully lighting up on the first try.

"Alex Adrian?"

"Insofar as he knows about you."

"I don't think he'll be any problem."

He accepted my judgment with a curt nod and closed his eyes against the curling smoke. "Tomorrow I shall make a nuisance of myself to Lieutenant Blair and see what his plans are concerning Adrian. He will have collected a number of reports on Sandra Robley's other friends by then, perhaps he will also have a better suspect upon which to focus his attention."

"I hope so."

"Indeed. I have serious doubts that the present judicial system would accept your unorthodox method of arriving at the truth as viable evidence."

"Especially since I'm not available during day sessions."

"I foresee another possible problem: You were with Adrian when he found the body. It is entirely possible you'll have to give evidence to that effect."

"Oh, shit."

"Or be held in contempt if you fail to show up."

"Couldn't I give a written statement or some kind of proxy?"

"I'm not sure, I'll talk to my lawyer about options. This was an occurrence I had not foreseen when I asked if you would like to work with me."

"Same here, but I was the one who asked you for help this time."

"I appreciate your confidence in me but fear it is misplaced this time. In essence, this is a tragic business, but of the sort that the police are best suited for dealing with."

"Even if they arrest the wrong man?"

He drew and puffed smoke, thinking carefully. "I doubt they will be able to scrape up a strong enough case against him to bring it to court. He has no alibi, to be sure, but he has that in common with a lot of people, including myself."

"Yeah, but you didn't know Sandra and you have no motive."

"True. Then who did? Who would want to kill such a woman? The violence preceding her death and the violent manner in which she was dispatched indicate that she aroused a great deal of emotion in her murderer. Who among her circle possesses such a temper?"

"Alex."

"Of course, always back to him, and you are absolutely certain of his innocence? Yes, then we must look elsewhere." He tapped the pipe against his teeth a few times and opened his eyes to look at me. "Do you fancy another outing tonight?"

"Where?"

"To the Robleys' flat."

"Any reason why?"

"Because I wish to have a better look at it. Circumstances were such that I had no chance for a good look 'round on the night of her murder."

Oh Lord, it looked like he was going into one of his energetic moods again. All I wanted to do was lie around the rest of the night and think about Bobbi. "Won't the cops have cleared away everything important by now?"

"I'm certain of it, but I wish to see what they deem unimportant." He put his pipe aside and stretched out of the chair, looking like a stork unfolding from its nest. "Charming as it was to entertain Miss Steler, I feel I've been vegetating here all evening. A drive in the cool air will do me a world of good."

"It's kind of late to be waking up the super in their building."

"I've no intention of disturbing that worthy man's rest."

"You need me along to go through the door and let you inside?"

"Not as long as I have my burgling kit. I would like your company because you had been there only a scant hour or so prior to the crime and can so inform me of any differences that might impress themselves upon your memory."

"After all this time?"

"You underestimate yourself, though I do see the point that for you, the period between has been amply filled with activity. Are you really that tired?"

An answer to that question might lead to a dozen other questions, none of which I wanted to go into at the moment. "I think I can last till morning."

"Excellent! I'll just fetch my keys—"

I stopped him before he got too far along. "Let's take mine, it's already warmed up, and I wanted to move it closer to the house anyway."

"Quite so. I daresay it will be less conspicuous in that neighborhood than my Nash." He tossed me my hat and settled his own at a rakish angle over his brow. Now that he had something to do he was impatient to be off, so I speeded up a little, but my heart wasn't in it. The next time Bobbi and I exchanged, I was going to make damn sure I had nothing else to do for the rest of the night but recover from the celebration.

Escott opened the front door and practically bounded down the steps. I moaned inwardly and did what I could to keep up.

We walked into the building normally. Escott was of the opinion that in this case stealth would draw more attention than if we acted like we belonged. No one bothered to poke their heads out as we climbed the stairs, and after a short moment of listening, I was satisfied no one would.

The police had sealed off the flat, which was hardly a barrier to me. I saved Escott the trouble of working with his skeleton keys and picks and went on through the door to open it for him from inside. He slipped in, shut the door quietly, and flipped on the light.

Sadness hung in the air like a fog. Things had been moved and shifted but not cleaned up. Fingerprint dust was still everywhere and the chalk outline still lay on the floor, a pathetic marker of her presence. Escott frowned furiously at it, shook his head sharply as if to clear his mind, and moved on to search the kitchen.

He did not take long and moved through the two small bedrooms and the bath just as quickly before coming back to the front again. "Does anything draw itself to your attention?" he asked.

"Evan's painting has been moved."

Apparently some fastidious soul had seen the big self-portrait at just the right distance and had turned it to face the wall. I reached for it.

"A moment." Escott had come prepared and gave me a thin pair of rubber gloves, the kind surgeons use. He was already wearing some himself, I just hadn't noticed when he'd put them on. I shook myself inwardly and tried to pull on an attitude of professional detachment along with the gloves. In this depressed state I was no good to anyone.

I tipped the painting out enough to see that it was undamaged and checked the other vertical racks and their contents. As far as I could tell, nothing was missing or marred, though as elsewhere, many of the paintings had fingerprint dust on them. Escott found that of interest and peered at the bright colors of an abstract through his pocket magnifier.

"It appears Mr. Robley used his fingers as well as his brushes to achieve certain effects."

"Sandra, too. Both of them had paint stains on their hands."

"Are these Sandra's?" He indicated another stack of stored paintings against the opposite wall.

"I guess so, we only looked at Evan's that night."

He sorted through them. "She would seem to be less prolific than her brother, as there is more than adequate storage space available—or perhaps she sold more?"

I nodded. "She said she was on some kind of WPA art grant. That was how they were able to live."

"Producing art for federal buildings?"

"Yeah. I think she also did stuff for interior decorators. There's apparently a market for genuine oil paintings."

"I've heard of it, assembly-line oils, pretty pictures for the masses at the cost of artistic integrity."

"Integrity is hard to afford when you don't have food in the cupboard," I pointed out.

"Yes, there are strong arguments in both directions, and who's to say where one may safely draw the line?"

That called for a second look on my part, but I didn't think he meant it as a pun. I flipped through Sandra's work with Escott looking over my shoulder.

"She would appear to have a wide range of styles," he said. "This one is after one school and this after another. I wonder if she ever had time to develop a style of her own. . . ."

"What do you mean?"

He set four different paintings out for view. "These for example: all are landscapes and all depict the same basic forms of hills, trees, and water, but they could have been painted by four different people. I'd be inclined to think so, too, but they are all out of the same palette." He darted to the other side of the room, where some painting supplies were kept, and drew out a thin flat of paint-stained wood, then held it up to the landscapes. The dominating colors of brown, green, and blue matched.

"You're sure about that?"

"I've had a smattering of art in my time. A painter's palette is often as identifiable as his fingerprints."

"Okay, so we know Sandra painted them all. Her work had to appeal to a lot of different people so she could sell. Is it important?"

"All information is important until proven otherwise." He returned the palette to its place and focused his attention on one of the big easels. "Is this one hers?"

"I think so."

He flipped off the dust cloth protecting the surface of the canvas beneath. The painting was an angular townscape in autumn, with wet streets and blowing leaves. Escott peered at it closely with his lens, then with his beaky nose practically touching the surface, sniffed. He backed off, puzzled, sniffed again, covering a wider area this time.

"What are you doing?"

"Checking the state of the linseed oil."

"Is it stale?" I asked, amused.

"Indeed." He swept the flat of one hand across the painting and held his clean palm up for inspection. "It's quite dry."

"Why would she have a dry painting on the easel?"

He didn't answer but went back to her store of paintings and flipped through them, rapidly pulling out three, all the same size. They showed the same angular street, with variations of color and light.

"Winter, spring, summer and the one on the easel is autumn, obviously a series on the theme of the four seasons. I suppose it is just possible she was doing a little touch-up work, but it hardly seems likely."

"Why's that?"

"Please note the top clamp of the easel: it stops a good five inches above the painting."

"Meaning that it was originally adjusted for a different-size canvas?"

"Exactly. Now I wonder what became of that particular work?"

"She could have taken it out herself."

"Then where is it? There are no wet paintings in this flat and she could not have sold them in that state."

"The cops took them."

He shook his head. "No, I stayed here and watched the forensic men. They did not remove any paintings. So unless Alex Adrian broke in and took them to his home for safekeeping or out of sentiment—"

"You figure the killer is some kind of art lover?"

"I'm not sure what to think. They were taken for a reason and unless he's mad enough to want to retain a most dangerous souvenir of his crime, the only reason I can think of to justify his theft is—"

"That what he took incriminates him in some way. Then what was it, a quick portrait or something?"

He had no answer for me and flipped the dust sheet back onto the canvas, then turned and brooded over the chalk scrawl on the floor.

It blocked my sight for only a moment, but I saw Evan again, standing in the same spot and swaying at the waist; Blair watching in shock, and Brett reaching to help him. That inhuman keening went through me once more and I shivered as though someone had walked over my empty grave.

Oh God.

Sometimes it happens that way, your mind hits on an answer with a sudden bright burst of insight, but won't tell how it got there, and you're left fumbling for an explanation. It eventually came tumbling out of my memory: words, looks, gestures . . . all fell together, linked up, and formed into a solid composition.

"Oh God." This time it slipped out aloud.

Escott sensed something in my tone. His eyes snapped up, silently demanding to know what it was.

I told him.

He soaked it up without comment, having heard some of it before, but only presented as idle conversation, and mixed in with other events. In the end he could only shake his head.

"You have the answer, and if we find the paintings, we'd have enough circumstantial evidence for the DA to bring it to trial—"

"But I sure as hell can't come to court to tell it. The one thing I can do, though, is get the written confession you wanted."

"Before only a single witness?" he questioned, meaning himself.

But I had a second witness in mind even as he raised the point.

12

THE STREETS WERE dead and sheeted over with cold white reflections from occasional lights. It was after midnight and one look at the lead gray sky clamped hard over the city was enough to make you realize how far away dawn could get if it really tried.

Escott sat next to the door and pretended to look straight out the windshield. Between us was Alex Adrian, who was doing the same thing, only he wasn't pretending. The stuff inside his mind was keeping him too busy. His face was drained and white, even the lips. His hands with their bandaged wrists were curled protectively around one another, the right thumb and finger twisting his wedding band back and forth in slow, unconscious rhythm. Except for that and the motion of the car, he was perfectly still. He could have been a corpse, right down to the invisible wall behind his eyes.

I'd asked a lot of him, and before things were finished I'd have to ask more—the question was, how much could he stand. He was an unexploded bomb now and I didn't know the length of his fuse.

"Turn here," he said. I nearly jumped—you don't expect a corpse to talk. "It's the servant's drive, better access," he added, his voice soft and distant.

I turned into a narrow break in the curb line. Trees crowded overhead and we rolled slowly along the drive's smooth cement surface for a hundred yards.

"Stop now and get out."

It wasn't a command, only another unemotional direction to follow. I eased the car to a halt and got out, pressing the door shut instead of slamming it. Adrian slid over on the seat, worked the gears, and drove off with Escott. They would circle around to the front of the stone castle Reva shared with Brett and use the main door. They'd called ahead and were expected company. I was not.

I followed in their wake. The driveway ran by a long slate-roofed garage with four wide doors and then curved away out of sight, masked by the bulk of the main house. The garage had two stories, but no lights were showing in any of the upper windows, so no chauffeur had been wakened by the passing of my Buick. The plain cement gave way to a span of decorative brick in a pattern, which I crossed to get to the house.

Except for a subdued night-light in the kitchen, the rest of the place was as dark as the garage, at least on this side. I found my way to the back garden and the line of French windows that marked the long hall where Bobbi had sung. The place was quiet enough now with all the people gone and looked larger than I remembered. The wind stirred unswept leaves around my ankles and I was just able to pick up the soft rush from the fountain at the far end of the grounds. It seemed like a century had passed since the night of the party, when I'd dragged Evan sputtering from the water.

Pressing my ear to one of the doors, I only heard the slow tick of a clock somewhere inside. The quality of the sound muffled, went silent a moment, and returned sharp and clear as I slipped into the house and became solid again. Oriented, I turned left and walked quietly through a series of rooms and halls, my ears cocked and the rest of me ready to vanish at a second's notice. The bedrooms were all upstairs, though. I didn't expect to run into anyone else prowling around and did not.

Like Adrian, Leighton Brett placed his studio on the north side of the house to take advantage of the light. It was a much bigger room and filled with more stuff, but had the same air of organized chaos. A line of wet canvases mounted on different kinds of easels took up a lot of floor space on one side. They covered many subjects: landscapes, some flowers with a jug, and the start of a bowl of fruit. The air was thick with the smell of linseed oil and the sickening bite of turpentine.

Operating on the principle of *The Purloined Letter*, I made for them and took a good look, comparing the colors of the canvases with the leftover smears on a palette I found. I was anything but an expert, but they seemed to match, which didn't prove much one way or another—Sandra had used the same colors. We'd probably have to wait and work it from the fingerprint angle later on, just to be sure.

I caught the low voices and approaching footsteps in plenty of time to vanish. Something clicked after the door swung open, probably the light switch, and they walked into the studio.

"The kitchen really might be better for this," said Leighton Brett. "At least I could offer you coffee or something stronger. I don't keep any supplies here where I work."

"We want nothing," stated Adrian, his voice toneless as ever.

"Then why are you here at this hour?" The question held no exasperation, only reasonable curiosity.

I moved close enough to Escott to give him a shiver and let him know I was around, then floated off a pace. The door was shut, very firmly and quietly, and Escott said, "We must talk."

"All right. About what?"

He did not get a direct answer. They were probably staring at him, reluctant to start now that the moment had come.

"Alex, what is this about?"

"Sandra's murder." This time there was some expression to Adrian's voice, more than enough to put Brett on his guard.

"Jack." But Escott didn't really have to call me, I was already fading into the room.

Brett went comically slack-jawed at this. A whimpering sigh of fear rushed from him and his pupils dilated, turning his eyes to black pits. I clearly heard the jump and throb of his heart. He stumbled away from me, grabbing at the back of a fancy brocade sofa for balance. I kept still and did my best to hold his eyes. They kept dancing from me to Adrian, to Escott, and back as he tried to take it in. I didn't dare look away to see how they were doing, I was completely focused on Brett.

His surprise died abruptly as common sense took over. He'd seen something impossible, therefore he hadn't really seen it. My appearance had been some kind of trick. He was desperate to believe this, I could read it on his face like print on a page. When he looked at me for some kind of tip-off or confirmation of the joke I had him cold, and he went blank and wide-eyed as a store-window dummy.

I kept my voice low and even and told him to sit down on the sofa. He did so. He wore scuffed loafers and some old paint-spotted pants. Neither of them went with the embroidered Chinese dragons crawling all over his green silk smoking jacket. Maybe it had been a present from Reva for some birthday or other.

He was tractable now and it was safe for me to divide my concentration. Escott was on the other side of the studio examining the paintings on the easels. Adrian regarded me with caution, but he was not really afraid.

"This is what you did to Evan?"

"More or less."

"How are you able to do it? Why?"

Escott and I had speculated on everything from telepathy to simple hypnosis, which my influencing resembled, and had yet to find a clear answer for how. *Why* I could do it was directly linked to vampiric survival: it was easier to drain blood from a quiescent source, whether animal or human, than from one awake and fighting the process. I shrugged; now was not the time for a lecture on my changed condition. Adrian let it go and sank into a chair opposite from Brett to stare at him.

I joined Escott by the paintings. "The colors looked alike to me."

"And they appear to be painted in Brett's style."

"You spot anything that could help?"

He was bent down behind one of the canvases and was comparing it to another he'd taken from a storage rack. "Indeed, yes, while not conclusive, it is certainly worth consideration. The wet painting's supporting frame is of a slightly different construction than the others in this room. It's homemade, while these came from a commercial supplier."

"Sandra and Evan made their own," said Adrian, not looking up from Brett's face. "They couldn't afford to buy prestretched canvas."

Escott peered at the raw edges of canvas through his magnifier. "The weave pattern of the fabric is also slightly different, but I believe—yes, there are some fingerprints in the paint. That will give us the final confirmation at least of the circumstantial element. As for the rest . . ." He broke off and replaced the dry canvas on the rack and went to stand just behind Adrian. I sat on the sofa, close to, but not touching Brett.

"I want you to speak freely and answer some questions," I told him. "You will give us the complete truth. You will tell us everything we want to know." I licked my dry lips and nodded to Escott, who leaned forward.

"Brett, did you take some paintings from Sandra Robley?"

"Yes."

"Why did you take them?"

"They were mine."

That puzzled him. "They were *your* paintings?"

Adrian spoke. "He means they were done in his style."

Escott noted that with a quirk of one eyebrow and continued. "Brett, did you kill Sandra?"

"Yes."

He spoke without hesitation, no emotion, no change in his empty face. I looked away from him and kept watch on Adrian. He was also leaning forward from his chair, a sullen fire burning deep in his eyes. Maybe it was hot enough to set off his fuse, maybe not. I was there to make sure the explosion wasn't too destructive.

"Why did you kill her?"

"She was . . . stealing from me." Now a long shudder

sieved through the big man's body and he seemed to shrink a little.

"What do you mean, stealing?"

"My life, all my work, taking it, using it."

Adrian stood up suddenly and crossed to the wet paintings. He glared at them, half reaching for them, then dropped his hands and swung back on Brett.

"You killed for this, because she imitated your—"

"Stole my vision and method, my ideas, and sold them for pennies," Brett whispered.

He stepped toward Brett and I tensed for the rush, but it did not come. It was less self-control than sheer disbelief that kept him from doing anything. He came closer, slowly, and stood over Brett. "Look up at me."

Brett looked up as ordered, with defiance creeping into his expression. My hold on him had slipped, but it didn't matter, he saw only Adrian. Escott and I were just part of the furniture.

"Try to understand, Alex, I worked hard to get here. It doesn't come easy for me, and then when I found out someone was imitating my style, capitalizing on it, using it, degrading it—"

"Stealing what you could have made on it?"

"Not just that—"

"No, it's worse for you, isn't it?" Adrian grabbed two fistfuls of Brett's silk jacket and hauled him to his feet, dragging him close to Sandra's paintings. "You wouldn't have killed her for just the money."

Brett didn't resist and only stared. Adrian released him, took out a landscape from the racks, and held it next to the one on the easel. Side by side you could see the difference. Brett's painting looked like the work of an imitator, Sandra's was the more expert piece.

"The money wasn't that important to you but your precious vanity couldn't take it. Anyone, even one with a crippled soul and no talent can see it. She copied your style because it's popular with the public, it sells, but she was *better* at it." He turned back to Brett. "She produced the kind of quality you could never hope to master, you knew it, you couldn't stand the thought of it.''

Brett slapped the back of his hand at Sandra's canvas, missing it by a fraction. "She was embarrassed at first—and then she *laughed*, tried to make a joke out of the whole thing. She asked if I minded very much, that maybe I should be flattered. . . .''

The muscles in his heavy face knotted into something unrecognizable and I knew what Sandra had seen the second before he struck her down. Adrian saw it, too, and sensibly kept his distance.

"*Flattered.*" He looked to be working into something I couldn't stop, unless I stopped it now.

"*Brett.*"

The interruption distracted him just enough. He looked at me and most of the tension left him, but none of the bile. "You helped, you know. You told me about those other paintings and where they were being sold from. I got Sandra's name from them—"

Adrian cut through the smoke. "Don't shift the blame, Leighton, he never told you to kill her."

He didn't like hearing that and shook his head as though the words physically hurt him. "I didn't mean to, I really didn't— you have to believe that . . .''

Adrian said nothing and turned away. He stopped before the studio door. "The only things I or anyone else can believe are your actions.''

"Alex, I am *sorry*. I lost my temper.''

"I'm sure the jury will be more than sympathetic," he murmured.

Brett didn't hear. "It got away from me. I truly am sorry, it was like before, I just couldn't help myself.''

Adrian's spine stiffened. "What did you say?''

"I . . . am . . . sorry.''

I got Brett's attention. "We know you're sorry, now tell us what about.''

His tone flattened from pleading to bald fact stating. "I'm sorry about Sandra . . . and Celia.''

Adrian turned, his face all caved in, and hell in his eyes. *"Celia?"*

My influence had put the chink in the dam. Brett's conscience, what he had of it, did the rest, and the dam broke at last.

"She said she wanted to go back to you. I told her you wouldn't change. You're like nails, Alex, all sharp points and iron outside, and nothing inside but more iron. What woman could love that? I tried to tell her."

Adrian made a glottal sound and swayed, but stayed on his feet.

"You knew what she'd done, I told her she'd already lost you, that it was too late anyway. She was *mine* by then—she wouldn't listen to me. She wouldn't admit it to herself and she was *wrong*, and I hated her for . . . then later, when I saw how you took it, how much you *did* love her, I was sorry, more than you'll ever know."

"You killed her?" His lips barely moved.

Brett's eyes stabbed around the floor for an answer. "She'd written me a note breaking it off, said she couldn't go on any longer. I told her it wasn't good enough and that I had to see her. I really tried, but she was in an awful state, and we'd both had a lot to drink. She just would *not* listen.

"I couldn't stand it, I was so damned angry with her—I just couldn't help myself. It was quick, she was passed out drunk when I took her home. I left her in the car along with the note. She suffered no pain. . . ." He trailed off and finally shut his mouth.

Adrian backed right up to the door, bumped against it, and scrabbled for the knob with stiff fingers. It twisted and he got the door open and went out, leaving it to swing free; a gaping hole leading into darkness.

I got in front of Brett and froze him to submission and gave him some very precise orders. Escott had taken a step toward the hall, but paused when I said his name.

"Stay here with Brett, I'll go."

He nodded and looked at his charge with more contempt than pity. It was still fresh on his mind that Brett had hired him to keep tabs on the progress of the murder investigation, and being used like that galled his professional pride. He moved toward Brett and put him to work.

Adrian hadn't gone very far. He was in some kind of sitting room down the hall. In passing, I just glimpsed his silhouette against the gray windows.

His palms were pressed flat to his eyes, with his fingers curled up over his forehead. He held his body erect, but was trembling all over as he fought for control and sanity against his grief and rage. After an endless moment the trembling lessened and stopped. The tension eased from the set of his shoulders and his hands fell away to hang forgotten at his sides. The walls were torn down and realization had flooded in. Perhaps he had known about Brett on some subconscious level, but had found it easier to blame himself for his wife's death than anyone else; things not our fault always are.

There was a sideboard on one wall with a half-full decanter and glasses. I poured out whatever it was and took it over to him. He accepted it without comment and drained the contents as smoothly as a glass of water.

"Did you know?" he asked. The pale curtains had not been drawn against the night and his eyes drifted aimlessly in the dim light seeping through the windows.

"Not about Brett and your wife."

He placed the glass carefully on a table. "I had to get out, it was that or kill him—and you wouldn't have let me."

"No."

"You saved me that humiliation, at least. Do you like what you do?"

"No, but it has to be done."

"And by whom? What are you? Is there a name for what you are?"

"Too many, and all of them ugly."

"Nemesis comes to mind. It's the wrong gender for you, but appropriate on this occasion."

"I'm sorry."

"Oh God, please don't start parroting Leighton."

"We had to have you along."

"Yes, I was the ideal choice to witness your wresting the confession from him. I can keep silent about your methods. Was there no one else?"

"It had to be you. You needed to know, to see."

"Did I?" His head came up sharply, but his gaze faltered after a second and eventually turned inward. "Yes, you're right again. You told me what to expect tonight, but you could have hardly anticipated this."

"I'd been looking for him, though."

"For Brett?"

"For your wife's killer, if he even existed."

"Perhaps I'm being obtuse. Would you explain?"

"I've still got a lot of reporter in me and it sticks. I checked the papers, talked to Barbara Steler—"

"Barbara?" He went cold on me again, or even colder, if that was possible. "What did you learn from her?"

"A sad story. She still loves you, you know."

He didn't believe me, which was hardly a shock.

"We had quite a talk, only she doesn't remember any of it."

His mouth twisted, bordering on disgust.

"That's how I learned that all the stuff about you killing your wife was so much eyewash. Barbara had been hurt pretty bad, it was her way of getting back at you."

"I already knew that."

"I think she knows she overdid it. She insisted on coming along the night you took on Dimmy Wallace."

"I never saw her."

"She didn't want you to."

"It's probably just as well."

I let the subject drop. "Anyway, I talked to a few people about you and your wife. The one thing that really got to me was that no one who knew you or even casually met you could believe you'd killed her."

"How generous of them."

"Then the chance came up for me to ask you directly."

"And just like Leighton, I told you the truth. Well, it's too late now to be offended by your curiosity. How did you come to realize she'd been murdered?"

"I didn't and I never did. I thought it was suicide like everyone else."

"Then why pursue it?"

I didn't want to tell him how I'd slipped back to his house and seen the portrait he'd done of Celia. I'd seen her through his eyes and the truth he'd recorded about her. Alex Adrian really had no conscious inkling of how deep his talent ran or the emotional effect it could have on others.

He'd painted the whole woman, her beauty, the guarded happiness, and the thin line of selfishness lodged in one corner of her mouth. In ten years that line would have taken over most of her face; in twenty, she'd have been quite ugly. The girl I had killed had been selfish, and I'd taken pains to make sure her death had looked like suicide. The parallel between her and Celia had gotten stuck in the back of my mind, so far back I hadn't thought of it until now. I hadn't wanted to think of it.

"Why?" he repeated.

Because by finding the truth behind one suicide and freeing Adrian of his guilt I could somehow expiate my own crime, or at least learn how to live with it as Gordy had advised me.

Because in my experience—and by now I did have experience—selfish people don't kill themselves. They have to have help.

Maybe my reasoning was screwy, I was feeling tired again. That made it easier to lie. "I don't know why, Alex. I just did, is all."

By now his eyes had grown used to the darkness and he was studying me closely. "There's more to it than that."

He was as perceptive in his own way as Escott, damn the man. I nodded. "Yeah, there's more, but it's only important to myself."

He believed me this time and knew I wasn't going to talk about it. He shrugged acceptance and glanced past my shoulder. "What are they doing in there?"

I shifted mental gears to bring myself back to the present, to the house I stood in now, and the people in it. "Brett's writing. I told him to do a full confession—on both murders. Escott's keeping an eye on him."

"That's good." His chin fell to his chest with sudden exhaustion.

"Alex . . ."

"What?"

"I can take the pain away; the memory will remain, but it won't hurt so much."

He thought about it and even raised his head a little. He knew what I was offering and could appreciate that I sincerely wanted to help. He was also aware I was giving him a choice in the matter. "I don't doubt that you could, I may even take you up on it—later. For now I can stand things—I've gotten used to it after all this time."

"It's not the kind of thing you want to hold on to."

"It will be exorcised soon enough—I'm not planning to kill myself, if that's what you think. I meant when we take him in to the police. Will this mean the death penalty?"

"I don't know."

"I hope it does." His eyes glittered unpleasantly and his mouth curled into a dry and bitter smile. "Don't you?"

He misinterpreted the answer in my face.

"Or is it too bloodthirsty of me to want a little justice?"

"I was only thinking this is going to be hell for Reva."

"She'll be better off without him," he said, dismissing the shattering of her own life with a casualness I didn't like, but could understand. "God, but I'm sick of it all and it's only just begun."

"You need sleep."

"I used to know what that was. I suppose you could fix that, too, as you did for Evan."

"Yeah."

"Evan." Some of the hardness went out of his manner.

"He gets out of the hospital tomorrow," I reminded him. "He's expecting to come here."

He looked pained. "Of course he can't come here, not after this. I'll have. to take him in for the time being and—" He froze. "Evan would have seen the paintings—unless Leighton planned to destroy them."

"If he wanted to destroy them he would have done so by now."

"Then why hasn't he?"

"You said the money wasn't that important to him. Maybe not, but Brett wasn't going to throw it away."

"He'd finish them and sell them as his own?" Adrian shook his head, trying to take it in.

"Evan wouldn't have been allowed to see them. Brett would have made sure of that. After the breakdown Evan had that night, no one would be too surprised if he took his own life. It's easy enough to arrange." I nearly choked on those last words, but he didn't know the real reason why.

"You knew all this?"

"Charles and I put it together as one of the possibilities. If the paintings hadn't been destroyed, we figured he had a reason to hold off. Greed was one of the ones we figured, it seemed plausible at the time."

"Leighton has everything already, how could he possibly want more? The money they'd bring in would be only pocket change compared to what he has. Why should he take such a risk?"

"Greed was just part of it. You hit on the real answer earlier. He doesn't have everything and he knows it."

He started to twist the wedding ring again, then stopped and looked at his hands. He held them flat, palms up. They didn't look like the hands of an artist, they were broad, the fingers blunt, but strong looking. Somehow they could transfer what he saw and felt onto paper and canvas in the manner that he desired. He could communicate his vision and emotion to others without spoken explanation. It was a gift, and perhaps by him it had been too long ignored or taken for granted.

"Sandra's talent," he stated.

"It's as you said; he'd finish them, sign them, and sell them—as his own. That's the key to all of it."

"Talent."

"Her paintings would have been his best work."

"The bastard," he said, with an odd uplift to his tone.

The DA got the verdicts he wanted, not that he had to work too hard with Escott practically handing him Brett's signed confession on a silver platter. Brett was found guilty of the first-degree murder of Celia Adrian and the second-degree murder of Sandra Robley, but avoided the death penalty in the end. He looked good in court and his obvious contrition impressed the judge and jury, if no one else.

Escott and Adrian were the prime prosecution witnesses, but they didn't have to work too hard at it, either. The facts concerning the murders were the bald truth, after all; the only lies had to do with how those facts were obtained. Escott gave the court a song-and-dance act about being suspicious of Brett's behavior the night Brett hired him to look into things. He later communicated his troubles to Adrian. When the two of them decided to ask Brett a few direct questions he quickly broke down and confessed. I'd made sure that Brett agreed with their story. It was a lousy one and I'd squirmed the whole time when we'd worked it out, but everyone swallowed it.

Escott wasn't too surprised. "They believe the most impossible things they hear on the radio and read in the papers every day. A simple little problem like this is hardly going to hold public attention for very long."

The papers were full of the story for a while, but mostly because of Alex Adrian's name. Escott and Adrian covered all the angles between them so my name never came into it, which suited me fine.

Brett's art at the gallery was sold off, and very quickly. The notoriety of the trial had drawn out collectors, thrill seekers, souvenir hunters, and other vultures. Because of the morbid competition, the paintings auctioned at premium prices. The money went to Brett's sister. Reva gave the gallery's commission to charity.

Things were tough for her, of course, though Escott was of the opinion she'd been more upset by Brett's affair with Celia than with his murders. After the trial, she went back east to stay with relatives until things cooled off, which they did, eventually. The next time we heard of her, she was re-opening the gallery, business as usual.

"What a resilient woman," Escott commented as he studied the article in the paper.

Evan came in with a tray of drinks. "And she's got good

taste to boot. She's promised she'll take on anything I might have to sell." He put the tray down and helped himself to a glass. "Maybe I should rephrase that, it sounds a bit rude."

"We know what you mean," said Bobbi, and that made him smile.

"I'm glad to hear she doesn't hold anything against you or Alex—or vice versa."

"It's not her fault that Leighton's a . . . well, that he's the way he is, and we all know that. She's better off without him, if you ask me," he said, unknowingly echoing Adrian's opinion from four months ago.

Christmas was only a week away and we were at Alex Adrian's house to pick up Bobbi's present.

"Anyway, it should be a success. She's got a head for the business, knows everyone worth knowing, and has the two best artists in the country to supply her with goods." Evan had aged a little in the last few months but was looking better tonight. He said he had a date coming by later, so apparently old habits were asserting themselves again and I was glad to hear it.

"Well, here's luck to all of you." Escott raised his glass and indulged in a sip, and the others followed his example. I kept out of sight in the back and faked it.

Adrian walked in and managed a smile. It was faint and a little self-conscious, but sincere. He still wore his wedding ring, but had dropped his habit of twisting it at about the same time he'd broken his painting block. "It's ready for view," he announced.

We followed him back to the studio. All the lights were on, blazing against an organized explosion of colors from every wall. Adrian was a busy man again, as much in demand as ever, but he'd found time to fulfill one private commission, and I was anxious to see it.

Bobbi's face was lit up with pride and excitement as Adrian flipped back the dust cover from her portrait.

Evan had promised that Adrian would do a painting that would knock our eyes out and he hadn't exaggerated one bit. Bobbi's vibrancy, beauty, and sensuality crackled off the canvas like electricity from a summer storm. It was the kind of painting that made you realize why people loved art for its own sake, but then it was by Alex Adrian, and I had expected nothing less than a masterpiece.

The one thing I didn't expect to see was myself in the painting as well.

"What gives?"

Bobbi laughed at my puzzlement, and now I understood all her suppressed excitement. "Merry Christmas, Jack."

Jeez, I never know what to say at happy surprises and started mumbling I don't know what idiocies.

"I think words are not necessary at this point, old man," Escott chided.

He was right, so I grabbed Bobbi and lifted her high and spun her until she shrieked for me to stop. Then I gave her a kiss and we looked at the painting again.

As in his original sketch, Adrian had her reclining on a low couch, loosely wrapped in some timeless white garment that clung to her figure. She looked like a slightly worldly angel about to become more worldly than heaven might want to allow. One hand rested along the top back of the couch and was covered by one of my own. I loomed over her in sober black, but he'd somehow managed to make me look ghostly and ethereal in comparison.

The background was dark, neutral chaos with my figure emerging out of the swirling non-pattern. Where my hand touched Bobbi's I was quite solid and real. It should have looked ominous and threatening, but did not. This was what he'd seen that night months back in the garage when I dived out of thin air to save his life. He'd said it had been beautiful and here he'd found a place to record his vision.

I held my hand out to him. He seemed surprised at the gesture, but shook it and finally smiled again. This one had more confidence.

"How do you do it?" I asked.

He decided to answer with more than a deprecatory shrug. "We're artists. We see and understand more than most because we've had to look at ourselves first—and accept what we find there whether we like it or not."

"It still doesn't make us any easier to live with," added

Evan. He stood back a little from the painting and compared it to the models. "I'm not sure I understand your symbolism, Alex, but it's certainly one of your best."

"There's no symbolism," Adrian assured him, keeping his face supremely deadpan. "I only ever paint what I see."